BEACON STREET GIRLS

This book belongs to:

VERITAS AMICITIA GAUDIUM
truth friendship fun!

™

Who's Who

Katani Summers
a.k.a. Kgirl ... Katani has a strong fashion sense and business savvy. She is stylish, loyal & cool.

Avery Madden
Avery is passionate about all sports and animal rights. She is energetic, optimistic & outspoken.

Charlotte Ramsey
A self-acknowledged "klutz" and an aspiring writer, Charlotte is all too familiar with being the new kid in town. She is intelligent, worldly & curious.

Isabel Martinez
Her ambition is to be an artist. She was the last to join the Beacon Street Girls. She is artistic, sensitive & kind.

Maeve Kaplan-Taylor
Maeve wants to be a movie star. Bubbly and upbeat, she wears her heart on her sleeve. She is entertaining, friendly & fun.

Ms. Razzberry Pink
The stylishly pink proprietor of the "Think Pink" boutique is chic, gracious & charming.

Marty
The adopted best dog friend of the Beacon Street Girls is feisty, cuddly & suave.

Happy Lucky Thingy and alter ego Mad Nasty Thingy
Marty's favorite chew toy, it is known to reveal its alter ego when shaken too roughly. He is most often happy.

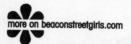
more on beaconstreetgirls.com

BEACON STREET GIRLS

Be sure to read all of our books:

BSG Special Adventure Books
charlotte in paris
freestyle with avery

First Edition

The characters and events in this book are fictitious.
Any similarity to real persons, living or dead, is coincidental and not
intended by the author. References to real people, events, establishments,
organizations, products, or locales are intended only to provide a sense
of authenticity, and are not to be construed as endorsements.

Series Editor: Roberta MacPhee
Art Direction: Pamela M. Esty
Book Design: Dina Barsky
Illustration: Pamela M. Esty
Cover photograph: Digital composition

Produced by B*tween Productions, Inc.
1666 Massachusetts Avenue, Suite 17
Lexington, MA 02420

ISBN: 0-9758511-9-5

CIP data is available at the Library of Congress
10 9 8 7 6 5 4 3 2 1

Printed in Canada

CR

Visit the Beacon Street Girls at beaconstreetgirls.com

lucky charm

PART ONE
DOG TROUBLE

CHAPTER 1

൭

RAIN, RAIN, GO AWAY!

"IS IT SUPPOSED TO RAIN tomorrow, too?" Avery asked. Her first sip of hot chocolate left her with a frothy white mustache. She licked it off with her tongue and grinned. Whipped cream was her absolute favorite topping.

Nick, who worked in his family's bakery after school and on some weekends, nodded toward the window. "Sorry, weatherman says it is."

"No!" Maeve gasped. "It can't. Tomorrow's the first day of the Brookline 300 Festival. I totally love street fairs."

"Will they cancel it?" asked Isabel.

"I doubt it," Nick said. "It's a rain-or-shine event."

"No one wants to go on rides in a downpour." Katani shook her head, disappointed.

"Don't worry. If it rains, you can stop at the Montoya's Bakery booth," Nick offered. "We'll have a ton of hot chocolate and warm apple cider. Of course, in the morning, we'll have fresh warm donuts and biscotti in the afternoon." He folded his arms and smiled.

Charlotte felt like he was looking only at her. *Maybe he'd be able to get away from working at his parents' booth long enough to go on a couple of rides with me*, she crossed her fingers as he walked away from the table.

"I really hope it doesn't rain. Everything would be ruined," Katani sighed. "I was looking forward to seeing how the craft people market their stuff. I thought maybe next year ... I mean, if I got my act together, I might be able to have a booth at the festival to sell my Kgirl accessories."

"Well," Maeve said, "if anybody our age could do that, it would definitely be you."

"Personally, I'm looking forward to the arcade games," said Avery, slurping her hot cocoa with her spoon. "I rock at the ball toss! And I heard they're going to have a real batting cage. I can't wait to try it out. In fact, it might be better if it does rain! Less of a line!" Avery picked up her spoon, held it like a bat, and pretended to hit a homerun.

"I adore carnivals," Maeve said with a dreamy sigh. "I just saw *Carousel* with Gordon MacCrae and Shirley Jones ..."

Avery dropped the spoon to the table. "Who?"

"Don't tell me you never heard of Gordon MacCrae and Shirley Jones!" Maeve was aghast.

"Is this one of your old-time black-and-white silent movie things?" Avery asked.

"No ... it's a musical. In Technicolor! I love the carousel scene ... it's dreadfully romantic. 'I hope I never fall in love on a carousel,'" Maeve quoted dreamily. "That is such a great old song."

"Promise me you won't sing tomorrow," Avery said. "It might improve your chances."

Maeve threw a piece of biscotti at a grinning Avery.

"Just promise me it won't rain tomorrow," Katani said.

"If it does ... I'll sing 'Singin' in the Rain' instead and

dance just like Gene Kelly," Maeve replied.

"You mean like the little elephant in the G.E. commercial?" Katani asked. "My sister Kelley loves that commercial. She doesn't watch programs, she watches commercials. The singing, dancing elephant is one of her favorites."

"I love that elephant!" Avery exclaimed.

"It's almost as cute as Gene Kelly," Maeve added.

"Who's she?" Avery asked.

"He!" Maeve stressed. "Geesh, Avery. Gene Kelly was a totally famous dancer and actor. Everyone in Hollywood knows him."

"Whatever, Maeve ... not everybody lives above a movie theater," Avery said.

"I don't want to do ANYTHING in the rain—and that includes singing," said Katani, who detested getting wet. "What about you, Charlotte? Will you go if it rains?" she asked.

Charlotte pondered this for a moment, then replied, "If it rains, I'll probably stay home and work on my article for *The Sentinel*. It's due in a week."

"That's not a bad idea!" Isabel said. "I have three cartoons due for the paper and I haven't even started thinking about them." Isabel's cartoons were a big hit in school. She even had a growing fan club that included several teachers.

"Did you get an interesting assignment for your article, Charlotte?" Maeve asked.

"Not really," Charlotte moaned. "I suggested a piece on that ninth grader Hilary Tamarack who's involved with the rescue of animals from hurricane areas. Her group rescued lots of dogs and cats and brought them to the Boston area in search of new homes after Hurricane Katrina."

"I heard about that," Avery said. "Those poor animals."

"I know," Maeve said. "It makes me think of how

horrible it would be if Marty were lost in a flood."

"There are thousands of lost and abandoned pets up for adoption. Maybe we should adopt a friend for Marty. What do you think, Charlotte?" Avery asked.

"I'm already pushing it with Marty, Ave," Charlotte said.

Marty, the Beacon Street Girls' mascot, was wiggly, cuddly, always getting into trouble, but so cute he got away with it—dog. The BSG found Marty in the park at the beginning of the school year when the girls were just getting to know each other. Avery wanted to keep him for herself, but her mother was allergic to dogs. That's how the little dude came to live with Charlotte in the first place.

"Boston rescuing hurricane pets—I think that's a really cool idea for your article," said Avery.

"Yeah, but I've been assigned a piece on the upcoming International Club dinner instead," answered Charlotte.

"How come?" Maeve asked.

Charlotte shrugged and looked down at her hands.

"Because," Isabel interjected, "Jennifer Robinson took the idea that Charlotte proposed. She wants to use it as the cover story, and SHE'S going to write it."

"No FAIR!" Avery growled.

"She can't do that," Katani said, slamming her hand on the table.

"She's the editor and an eighth grader," Charlotte said with a shrug, "so she gets to decide who writes what."

"Well, I think it's kind of mean of her," huffed Maeve.

"I think …" Isabel stumbled for words, "… I think Jennifer is a little jealous of Charlotte if you ask me. And I bet she's embarrassed because Ms. Rodriguez said she was disappointed with the quality of the writing from the eighth-grade staff, except she was full of praise for Charlotte."

"Really?" Maeve's eyes widened. "Our little Charlotte. Pray tell … what did Ms. Rodriguez have to say?"

"Maeve!" Charlotte wasn't sure she wanted everyone to hear the story, but Isabel was already telling what happened.

"Well, Ms. R likes to recap the most recent issue at the beginning of our *Sentinel* meetings. Also, she tries to focus on one aspect of journalism. Well, last time, we focused on interviews. She said that Charlotte was the only one who had nailed the assignment."

"Well … that's not exactly how she put it …" Charlotte said, blushing.

"No, what she actually said was that everyone could learn a lot from the only seventh-grade feature writer," Isabel proudly reported.

Charlotte could feel her ears burn bright red from embarrassment, but she also felt a rising swell of pride inside.

"Really? She said that?" Katani asked.

"Yeah. Jennifer was steaming," Isabel said.

"Oh?" Charlotte asked. "I missed that."

Isabel turned to Charlotte. "That's because you were sitting behind her," Isabel said. "It was pretty obvious that she was … well, jealous. She then gave Charlotte what she thought was the worst assignment for the last issue. She told her to interview the janitor," Isabel explained.

"And the article turned out to be awesome," Maeve said.

"Yeah," Katani said. "Mr. Hewitt is an interesting man. I can't believe he flew in a B-17 during World War II and helped build the World Trade Center in the seventies."

"I think that's why she took your new idea for herself," Isabel noted.

"Well, whatever her reason, I have to find a way to make the International Club dinner sound exciting," said Charlotte.

"So, let me get this straight. You're not going to the festival if it's still raining?" Avery asked.

"I didn't say that. I said MAYBE I'd work on my article instead," Charlotte clarified.

"Well, I think we should go rain or shine, like Nick suggested," Avery added.

"I guess if I wore something a little more weather-friendly, it wouldn't be too bad," Katani said, inspecting her pants for watermarks.

"Come on … who cares? What's a little rain? I mean none of us is going to melt or anything," Avery retorted.

"Not unless you're the Wicked Witch of the West," Maeve pointed out.

"And we're not," Isabel responded quickly.

"We should definitely get there early!" said Maeve.

"Yeah! Before all the donuts are gone," Avery suggested.

"Good idea," agreed Charlotte.

The girls gathered up their things and headed for the door.

As Maeve buttoned up her raincoat and stuffed her red hair into the hood of her jacket, she started humming "Singin' in the Rain."

By the time they were ready to leave, all the girls were humming madly.

"Can I borrow your umbrella?" Maeve asked Charlotte.

Curious, Charlotte handed it over. And before she knew it, Maeve jumped into a Gene Kelly dance sequence. She hooked the end of the umbrella around the lamppost, swung around the post, and deftly landed back onto the sidewalk.

"Let me try that," Avery said holding out her hand.

Katani looked down at her wet pants in dismay. "Can we save the dance lessons for a time when it's NOT pouring out?" she asked.

"OK … OK … just one more …" Avery said, swinging out over the gushing water and landing easily back onto the sidewalk. "You try it, Charlotte."

"I don't think …" Charlotte started.

"Come on, it's easy!" Avery did it again.

Charlotte had to admit that it did look easy and fun, too. She grabbed the closed umbrella and hooked the end around the light pole. Launching herself across the water, she swung up and out. But, the umbrella slid down and off the pole, and Charlotte toppled into the gutter and the rushing water with a splash.

"Oh gosh! Charlotte, are you all right?" Maeve asked, kneeling on the curb.

"So much for singing in the rain," Charlotte said as the water swirled around her. "I'm singing in the gutter." The klutz-factor had kicked in again. Unfortunately, not only was Charlotte sitting in a torrent of water, but when she looked up she could see Nick standing in the window of the bakery watching her. Yikes! Somehow that boy always seemed to catch her at the worst possible moment.

"Come on … let's get Twinkle Toes out of the gutter and on her way home to dry clothes," Katani giggled, offering Charlotte her hand. Isabel rushed forward and the two of them hauled Charlotte out of the gutter.

Charlotte didn't dare look back at the bakery window. She hoped that by now Nick was taking an order or washing down the counter or doing SOMETHING else besides watching her humiliating escapade.

Breathe, breathe, Charlotte. No one ever died from embarrassment, Charlotte whispered under her breath. Did they?

This was something her father told her all the time. He

had to be right, because if people died of embarrassment, she would have died back in France when the billy goat tore the bottom from her pants ... and she had to walk home from school with everyone knowing she had on days-of-the-week underwear that said "Sunday"—and it was Wednesday!

❧

CHAPTER 2

NO FAIR!

KATANI WAS SURPRISED to find herself in an empty house when she arrived home. Her Grandma Ruby, the principal at Abigail Adams Junior High, had stayed late at school with her sister Kelley. Her parents were both still at work, and her sister Patrice was probably at basketball practice. "Wow, it's all mine." She hugged herself and twirled around.

Katani was the youngest in a family of four girls. Her family sometimes teased her about being the baby, which was funny because Katani was the tallest of them all. Even though she was the youngest, Katani sometimes felt that she had the most responsibility. After all, she was the one who spent more time looking after her sister Kelley than anyone. Not only did they both go to the same school, but they also shared a room. When Avery first heard about Kelley being autistic, she'd rolled her eyes and said, "Yeah, I hate being around those artsy types."

"Not ARTISTIC," Katani stressed. "AUTISTIC."

Then Katani had patiently tried to explain to her friends about a disability that even the experts still don't completely understand. She always described it the way Grandma Ruby did. As we grow, most of us learn to filter out most of the things our senses pick up. That way we can learn to focus on what's important to us. Autistic people have a faulty filter system. They live in a blizzard of sights, sounds, smells, and textures, so ordinary situations can become very overwhelming. Kelley was especially sensitive to sound and color.

Katani loved colors, but too much color made Kelley jittery. So Katani and her mother had fashioned pretty canvas blinds that rolled up and down to go over Katani's bookshelves to cover her collection of bright objects and books. On days like this when Kelley was away, Katani couldn't wait to pull up the roller shades, crank up the stereo, and really enjoy her room ... by herself!

She pulled out her favorite Beyoncé CD, turned up the volume, and rocked out. Even though she wasn't the world's greatest dancer, she loved to go crazy in the privacy of her own room. Katani had turned up her stereo so loud that she could feel the music through her feet. She danced her way to her closet to find the perfect outfit for tomorrow. Well, actually, two perfect outfits for tomorrow: one for rain and one for sunshine. *If it does rain, I'll look great. If it doesn't, I'll look even better!* she thought proudly.

"Katani! Katani!" Mrs. Summers called from the door. Too busy dancing and sorting through her jewelry for the perfect accessories, Katani didn't hear her mother call.

When she felt a tap on her shoulder, she jumped a mile. "Katani, we're home!" Mrs. Summers shouted over the music. "Turn the music down and ..." She nodded to the bookshelves.

"Oh, Mom! I just got here! Can't I just have a few minutes in my own room ... all by myself?"

Mrs. Summers didn't have time to answer. Even over the

loud music, Katani could hear her sister, Kelley, skipping down the hallway. When Kelley appeared at the door, she instantly clapped her hands over her ears. "Too loud! TOO LOUD!" she screamed.

Katani reached over and snapped the volume down on the song just when it was getting to her favorite part. Katani thought it was ironic that Kelley was sensitive to sound, since she was usually the loudest one in the house.

Mrs. Summers edged closer to Katani. "Your sister's a little … agitated this afternoon so …" she nodded again to the shelves.

"Why can't I have my own room with a lock on the door?" Katani mumbled to herself as she lowered the blinds. "None of my friends have to worry about not having colorful posters or keeping their stereos turned down."

Kelley's side of the room was lit by soft bulbs that muted the colors in the room. Katani hated the red light bulbs. They made her feel like she was living on Mars. Katani was hanging her clothes back in the closet when her mother's cell phone rang. Mrs. Summers took the call in the hall, but Katani overheard enough of the conversation to know that her mother was irritated.

"Great, that's just what I need," Mrs. Summers said, pulling her PDA from her worn, brown briefcase and entering in an appointment.

"A deposition … tomorrow morning. How inconvenient! That really cuts into my family time. I'll have to rearrange my entire schedule. That means I'll have to shuffle some things around." She clicked off her phone and turned to Katani. "I'm sorry honey, but I need you to walk Kelley to her physical therapist tomorrow morning."

"Oh, Mom, I can't tomorrow. It's the first day of the

Brookline 300 Festival."

"You can go on Sunday," Mrs. Summers suggested.

"But my friends are all going tomorrow. We have PLANS."

"Well your plans are just going to have to change," Mrs. Summers said matter-of-factly.

"Mom! That's SO unfair!"

"I'm sorry, Katani, but your father is working overtime, Grandma Ruby has her optometrist appointment tomorrow, and Patrice has basketball. Even if Kelley didn't have an appointment, you would have had to stay home with her."

Katani groaned. Why did she have to be the responsible one? It just wasn't fair that she always had to be so grown up, especially when Kelley was her older sister.

"So, how am I supposed to get to the physical therapist's office? Take a cab or something?" Katani asked.

"No, you can walk. We're seeing a new physical therapist, and her office is only a couple of blocks away. These appointments usually last an hour and a half, but this one might take a little longer. They are finishing up assessing Kelley's strengths and weaknesses. Last week it took more than three hours."

"Three hours! I have to stay there three hours?"

"It probably won't take quite that long, and I promise you, honey, I will do my best to get there before she's finished. I need to meet with the therapist after her appointment anyway. It would help to have you there. I have another deposition tomorrow afternoon, so as soon as the appointment is done, I'll need you to walk your sister home again."

Katani threw up her hands. "This is definitely not fair."

"Be thankful for all the gifts you have, Katani," Mrs. Summers said in a very low voice. "I'm certain Kelley would give anything to be as lucky as you and your sisters are."

Katani could hear Kelley rummaging through the kitchen.

She knew that her mother was right. But, it was just so hard some days to have Kelley for a sister. Kelley was really out of sorts today. Katani heard her mom moving about the laundry room, which was off the kitchen. Mrs. Summers was chucking an old tennis shoe and blanket into the dryer and turning it on air. For some reason, curling up with Mr. Bear on top of the dryer as it clunked and rocked made Kelley feel calmer. It was so effective that Grandma Ruby had even considered having a dryer installed at school.

Katani sunk back on her bed. She did feel sad for Kelley. Her sister would never go to college, never drive a car, or be a completely independent adult. And Kelley would always need help from other people.

Katani looked over at the two outfits lying on her bed. She had worked hard to find the perfect ensemble for tomorrow, and now it didn't even matter. Rain or shine— Katani Summers would be playing babysitter to her older sister. It was a fact. Her fun, relaxing weekend was ruined.

Chat Room: BSG　　　　　　　　　　　　　　　　 _ □ X

File Edit People View Help

Kgirl: change of plans. i'm out for tomorrow

flikchic: what?!?!?

4kicks: no way!

lafrida: what's going on?

Kgirl: gotta take sis to pt

skywriter: pt?

Kgirl: physical therapy

lafrida: 2 bad—I'm sorry

4kicks: u'll miss the batting cage

flikchic: u'll miss shoppng

Kgirl: don't rub it in

lafrida: it lasts all day?

Kgirl: no. only in a.m.

flikchic: so join us at noon

Kgirl: not sure that's a good idea

4kicks: y not?

skywriter: c'mon Kgirl better late than never

Kgirl: not that simple. i'd have to bring kelley along

4kicks: great!

lafrida: what's the problem?

flikchic: the more the merrier

skywriter: where should we meet?

5 people here

Kgirl
flikchic
4kicks
lafrida
skywriter

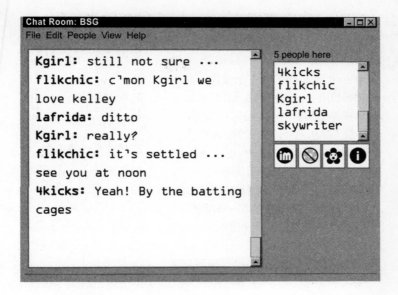

```
Chat Room: BSG                                    _ □ X
File  Edit  People  View  Help

 Kgirl: still not sure ...        ▲   5 people here
 flikchic: c'mon Kgirl we              4kicks          ▲
 love kelley                           flikchic
                                       Kgirl
 lafrida: ditto                        lafrida
 Kgirl: really?                        skywriter       ▼
 flikchic: it's settled ...
 see you at noon                      🄸🄼 🚫 ✿ 🄸
 4kicks: Yeah! By the batting
 cages
                                  ▼
```

TO GO OR NOT TO GO

All through grade school, Katani rarely had friends over. No play dates, no working together on science projects, no slumber parties. That was because Katani could never be sure what Kelley might do or say. Until this year, most of Katani's friends were frightened by Kelley's outbursts.

But now, for the first time in her life, Katani wasn't embarrassed to bring friends home. The BSG truly understood about Kelley and her autism. And Kelley was comfortable around the BSG. When she saw them in the hall at school, Kelley always wanted to hug them. When they came over to the house, Kelley wanted to play with them. Somehow it worked out OK.

Katani was pleased that her sister had started to feel comfortable around the Beacon Street Girls. But at the same time, she really wished that she could have something all to herself. It was enough that she had to share her room and the responsibility; she didn't want to have to share her friends all the time with her sister too. But Katani was OK with having to make some sacrifices for Kelley—that was just what you did for family.

Katani leaned back on her bed and stared at the outfits she picked out to wear to the festival tomorrow. She knew she was feeling crabby, but she just couldn't help herself.

"Well … they can't have it both ways," she muttered to herself. "They can't insist that I include Kelley and then suddenly decide that I *can't* include her."

A small voice inside cautioned her that taking Kelley to the festival could be trouble. If Kelley couldn't handle noise or the colors of Katani's room, how was she going to handle a festival? Hello! Sensory overload!

Katani focused on convincing herself that taking Kelley to the festival was the right decision. After all, having "age-appropriate peer social interaction"—which was often what Katani's parents said when they wanted Katani to include Kelley in her activities—would be good for Kelley.

CHAPTER 3

∝

DETAILS, DETAILS

MARTY JUMPED ON THE BED at precisely 6:43 a.m. Saturday morning and pawed at Charlotte's arm. It was barely light yet.

Charlotte moaned and rolled over. She liked it better when it was light at six in the morning.

Marty didn't care whether it was light out or not. He wanted to go out and he made that very clear to Charlotte by licking her on the face. When she covered her face with her arm, he resorted to nipping and pulling at the sleeve of her fuzzy pajamas.

"OK. OK! I get the message!" Charlotte relented, throwing back her covers.

Marty danced around Charlotte's feet as she pulled on her sweats, threw on the blue denim jacket that used to be her mother's, and headed down the stairs. Even though she tiptoed quietly, the old stairs creaked and groaned as if she were a two-ton elephant.

Marty didn't care about being quiet. His little toenails clicked on the wooden steps as he scampered down the stairs.

"Shh! Marty! Let's not wake up the whole house!" Charlotte scolded as she clipped the leash on Marty's collar and pushed out the front door into the chilly morning air.

The sky was a bit cloudy, but to the east there was nothing but blue. The rain, which had plagued the girls all week, had finally come to an end. *What glorious timing*, thought Charlotte as she headed toward the park. By the time she was on the field, the sun broke through the clouds and hung low over the Charles River.

But the rain had left its mark. By the time Charlotte and Marty made it home, the little dude's tiny paws were caked with mud and wet grass. Charlotte bent down and wiped each paw on the towel she kept by the door for that specific purpose.

"Someday, I'm going to teach you how to wipe your feet on the welcome mat," she said. Charlotte had an hour before she was supposed to meet the BSG (minus Katani) for breakfast, so she sat down at her desk to brainstorm ideas for her article.

At yesterday's meeting, Ms. Rodriguez reminded the *Sentinel* staff to avoid the passive voice and to use strong verbs and telling detail. "Good writers use their eyes *and* ears when gathering material for a story," Ms. Rodriguez told them. Then she asked, "What's in your notebook?" Charlotte prayed Ms. R wouldn't march down the aisle and flip open *her* notebook only to see there wasn't much but a few doodles and a note to do her social studies assignment.

Ms. R said good reporters think about their stories and seek out angles and details to draw their readers in. "Does your notebook just have stats? Facts? I want to see more than that! Be thinking as you are writing. Write down key words. Write down questions you want to explore further. Be curious. Good writing starts in your reporter's notebook,

NOT on the keyboard."

Charlotte couldn't remember Ms. Rodriguez ever being so impassioned. When Charlotte flipped through her skimpy notes, it was as if Ms. Rodriguez had been describing HER notebook. Charlotte decided right then and there that she was going to get a real reporter's notebook—the long, skinny kind that she could easily slip into her back pocket. The kind that she could easily hold in the palm of her left hand and write on with her right hand, just like a professional newspaper reporter.

Charlotte promised herself she was going to sharpen her observation skills to notice sights and sounds. She would look at people's expressions and how they moved. She needed to practice gathering what Ms. Rodriguez called "telling details." The Brookline 300 Festival would be the perfect place to practice.

Charlotte figured she might as well head to the festival early. "There's no time like the present to work on my reporting skills," she muttered, putting on her denim jacket. She grabbed her French mesh market bag. It was chic, as Katani had told her, but it was also expandable. Perfect for holding treasures. Maybe there'd be some really cool things at the fair today.

Marty danced at her feet. "Poor little guy," Charlotte said, bending down and scratching him behind the ear. You've been cooped up inside too much because of this nasty ole rain, haven't you? I know how you feel. I think it's going to be a great day. Want to come along?"

Marty yipped, excited by the spontaneous invitation.

Charlotte grabbed Happy Lucky Thingy at the last minute and threw it in her bag ... just in case. Happy Lucky Thingy was Marty's favorite chew toy and sort of like a dog pacifier. Charlotte wrote a note to her dad, clipped the leash on Marty, and headed out the door.

GREAT BEGINNINGS

The old-fashioned bell over the door rang as Charlotte entered Irving's Toy and Card Shop. Charlotte knew just what she wanted. She walked in past the racks of cards, past the display of newly arrived holiday toys, and headed straight to the stationery section in the middle of the store.

"And how are you on this beautiful morning, Charlotte?" the storeowner, Ethel Weiss, asked from the counter.

"I'm really great, Mrs. Weiss, how about you?"

"I'm so glad it's not raining today. I want to walk to the festival later."

Charlotte turned to Mrs. Weiss. *Use your observation skills*, she reminded herself. Mrs. Weiss wore oval glasses that magnified her eyes, which were a beautiful, clear hazel. "Can I help you find something?" she asked as she dumped penny candy into the jars.

"I was hoping to find a reporter's notebook. I know I've seen them here before," Charlotte said, scanning the shelf.

"Reporter, huh? So are you a budding Lois Lane? No, no … more the Woodward and Bernstein type, huh?" the proprietor asked.

"I … uh … don't know."

"Woodward and Bernstein were investigative reporters during President Nixon's administration … secret sources, cloak-and-dagger stuff … unraveling mysteries with a sharp mind and number-two pencil," Mrs. Weiss said, as she handed Charlotte a reporter's notebook.

Charlotte smiled. Mrs. Weiss had her own unique way with words. Charlotte liked the way she put ideas together.

She couldn't wait to record what Mrs. Weiss had said in her new reporter's notebook.

"Going to the festival? No?" Mrs. Weiss asked.

"Yes, I'm actually on my way."

"It should be a great day!"

"A really great day," Charlotte echoed, thinking it was too bad that Katani wasn't going to be able to join them until noon. She handed Mrs. Weiss money for the notebook.

"You are taking little Marty with you?" Mrs. Weiss asked, motioning toward the little dude, who sat patiently waiting for Charlotte to finish her purchases.

"Yes, he needs a day out. Poor little guy has been stuck inside all week because of the rain," Charlotte said.

"Haven't we all!" she said, handing Charlotte her change.

Charlotte thanked Mrs. Weiss and waved good-bye.

The BSG were supposed to meet at the fairgrounds outside Montoya's booth at ten. Charlotte was forty-five minutes early so she sat down on a bench and opened her notebook to write.

Charlotte began by writing quick two-sentence descriptions of the people that passed her as she sat on the bench. She'd filled up three pages before Isabel arrived.

"I think I know what you're up to," Isabel said as she sat down next to Charlotte.

"Yes," Charlotte said, flipping her new reporter's notebook closed and sticking it in her back pocket. She blushed. "I was just practicing."

"I did some brainstorming for my cartoons, too, but I'm still stuck for an idea. But, you know me, the last-minute pressure will get my creative juices flowing. It always does."

Maeve and Avery appeared, and smiles erupted on their faces as Marty bounded toward them.

"Give me a hug, you handsome little thing," an exuberant Maeve squealed, bending down to greet Marty.

"Marty, my man!" Avery exclaimed as she rushed to him. "Give me five, dude!" She squatted down in front of him and held out her hand.

Avery had been trying to teach Marty for months to raise his paw and slap her hand. Instead, Marty lunged at Avery, and she toppled to the ground. Marty hopped on her chest and began licking her face.

Avery didn't seem to mind at all, but Charlotte was embarrassed. People were staring. She reached down and helped pull Avery to her feet.

"The delicious smell coming from Montoya's booth is way too much for me to handle," Avery said. "What does a girl have to do to get a donut around here?" In no time, the girls were equipped with hot chocolate and warm cinnamon donuts.

Charlotte wanted to be able to write about how great the donuts smelled, but she was so hungry, she just couldn't wait. She bit into the soft, still-warm donut. Was there anything better? She tried to think of what words she could use to describe the experience so that when readers read her words, their stomachs would rumble, their mouths would water, and they would instantly crave one.

She was beginning to understand what Ms. Rodriguez had meant by "telling detail." It wasn't enough just to flesh out a story with words that took up space. The words had to be based on details ... what did she call them ... oh, yes ... *salient* details that made the dull, lifeless words come alive so that the reader felt like they were there!

"Charlotte, hurry up!" Avery said. "Stop writing and finish eating. If we don't hurry, there'll be a line at the batting cages."

"You and your batting cages," Charlotte shook her head.

When she stood up she noticed that some donut crumbs had landed in her hair. Just as she began to brush them out, she looked over and saw Nick waving to her from behind the counter at the bakery booth. *Figures*. Charlotte quickly wiped the sugar from the corners of her mouth, trying to appear nonchalant.

"Hey. Can I take control of the little guy?" Avery asked.

"He's all yours." Charlotte carefully handed over Marty's leash. She'd somehow managed to keep from tripping over the leash all morning, but now that she was in sight of Nick, anything could happen.

"Avery, wait!" Charlotte called as Avery trotted off. "I brought Happy Lucky Thingy—just in case he starts getting restless." Marty's favorite chew toy was always good to have on hand when they took Marty on an adventure.

"Thingy is starting to look a little sketchy!" Maeve said.

Isabel nodded. "I think he needs a dry cleaning. Or maybe we should replace him," Isabel said.

"Happy Lucky Thingy is Marty's favorite toy. Think about the sentimental value," Avery added. Happy Lucky Thingy was the only toy that Avery brought with her from Korea when her parents adopted her as a baby.

"But look at him, Avery. Marty has 'loved' Happy Lucky Thingy's happy face and mad face so much—you can't tell which side is which," Isabel laughed.

"I see what you mean, but we can't get rid of his toy. It would be like Charlotte not having her mom's denim jacket," Avery insisted.

"OK. Fine, but let's get going." Maeve was itching to start circulating at the festival.

Avery jammed Happy Lucky Thingy into her sports bag, and she and Marty dashed off down the path.

"Hey Avery, slow down!" Maeve called. "I want to look at some of the vendors."

"Wait up!" Charlotte called.

"Look, there's Razzberry Pink," Charlotte said to Isabel.

Razzberry Pink's booth was the standard white canopy, but she had dressed it up with a dozen shades of pink. Draped around the edges were all kinds of specialty lights hanging from the canopy—pink flamingos, pink elephants, and tons and tons of pink twinkle lights. Just like at her shop, Think Pink, there was a wide array of pink goods, but prominently displayed was a T-shirt with paw prints all over it.

Maeve found a pair of pink sunglasses with pink glitter at the edges and slipped them on. "Good morning, dahlings," she said dramatically in her best movie star voice. "They're just right for me, don't you think?"

"Good morning BSG," Ms. Pink said with a contagious smile. "I know just how to put you in the pink this morning. How about a Brookline T-shirt? The proceeds help benefit the local pet shelter. And look: It's pink!"

"Thanks, but we're just looking for now," Isabel said.

Marty woofed and wagged his tail.

"Hey! I know this little guy," Ms. Pink said. "He's Klondike Pink … right? Last time I saw this pup, he had on pink earmuffs and a pink scarf."

"Please … leave the man some dignity!" Avery said as she walked away from Ms. Pink's booth. The girls waved good-bye and continued on their way.

Like Razzberry Pink's, most of the booths set up along the main section of the fair were donating a small portion of their profits to various Brookline charitable organizations like the homeless shelter, the soup kitchen, meals on wheels, or the animal rescue project run by Dr. Barlow for a local pet shelter.

"Whoa! Look over there!" Maeve exclaimed. She pointed at a man wearing a baseball hat and a Red Sox jersey.

"You mean that really cute, tall, dark, and handsome guy?" Isabel asked.

"That's not SOME guy," exclaimed Avery. "That's the new Sox phenom, Robbie Flores."

"Who? Flowers? What?" Maeve asked.

"Not flowers, silly. Flores. What planet are you from, Maeve?" Avery asked.

"Planet Hollywood," Maeve shot back with a huge smile.

"Well ... Miss Hollywood, the rest of us in Boston know that that guy right there is the rookie right fielder on the fast track to being the Rookie of the Year because of his amazingly powerful bat."

"OH," Maeve said, eyeing the right fielder.

"He's batting over .325 this season and has 75 RBIs," Avery said.

"What's an RBI?" Charlotte asked.

"Runs Batted In ... Hello! I thought you were all loyal Red Sox fans?"

"I am!" Charlotte asserted. "I just don't really know the right words or all the players yet."

"Well ... I still have a soft spot in my heart for the Tigers," Isabel added.

Avery was outraged. "The Tigers! They're at the bottom of the league!"

"Yeah, but in Detroit, they are as loved as the Red Sox are in Boston," Isabel argued. "My dad says to wait until next season. They're in a rebuilding year."

"More like a massive rebuilding decade," Avery said, rolling her eyes again.

"I thought I heard the guys at school say something

about Robbie Flores being in a slump," Charlotte said.

"Hmmm ... well, he was doing great. I mean until about two weeks ago." Avery sounded concerned for her favorite Red Sox player.

"So is this guy a phenom or a lovable loser?" Isabel asked.

Charlotte thought that Isabel asked a valuable question. But no one else seemed to be paying attention.

"Robbie Flores is NOT a loser." Avery protested. "When he was hitting well, the Sox were on track for the playoffs. Now ... well ... that's up in the air, and this guy may be on a bus back to Rhode Island."

"Rhode Island? Is that where he's from? He looks South American," Maeve said.

Avery gave her a look. "Pawtucket, Rhode Island, is where the Red Sox Triple-A minor league team is located. The PawSox, Hollywood brain. Hey! Where did he go?"

The girls turned and looked. Robbie Flores had disappeared into the growing crowd.

"This place is a zoo—I better get to the batting cages and get in line. Come on little guy." Avery picked up Marty. "It's real easy for us short people to get trampled, so let's put you in my duffle for a while."

With Marty's head sticking out of her duffle bag, Avery made her way toward the batting cages. Halfway there, Marty began barking and pawing to get out. Avery rummaged around inside until she found Happy Lucky Thingy.

"Ruuussss!" Only muffled sounds came from the duffle bag now as Marty settled in to chew on his Happy Lucky little toy.

Katani glanced at her watch. Luckily, Kelley's appointment had been the first one of the morning. But it was 11:15 and her mother still hadn't shown up, and Kelly would be done any minute now. *This was nerve-wracking,* Katani fumed. She was supposed to meet the BSG at noon. Her mother always told Katani how important it was to be on time, but Mrs. Summers often ran late herself. Although, it wasn't her fault. Usually, a phone call from the office would snag her just as she was walking out the door.

Katani could just imagine her mother sitting behind her desk, still talking on the phone. On a Saturday, the one day when Katani should be free to do anything she wanted. The one day for her to kick back with her friends.

Katani looked at her watch again. Where was her mother? Katani was growing impatient. Just as she was trying to decide what to do, she looked up to see her mom walking through the door.

"Hi, honey," Mrs. Summers said, giving her youngest daughter a big kiss on her forehead. "Sorry I'm late."

Katani breathed a sigh of relief. "That's OK, Mom. Kelley is doing great. The therapist came out and told me." On cue, the door opened and the therapist beckoned for Mrs. Summers to come in. Before she entered the office, her mom reached into her briefcase and pulled out a magazine, which she handed to Katani. Katani smiled. It was *Scene*—her favorite.

Hopefully, her mom's meeting with the physical therapist wouldn't take too long. Katani flipped through the magazine as her mother talked. She wasn't purposely trying to overhear the conversation between her mother and Kelley's new therapist, but it was hard not to.

"Her fine motor skills are coming along, but she still

✿

needs help with her gross motor skills," the physical therapist explained.

Katani yawned. She'd heard her parents and grandmother discuss various therapies for years. Kelley saw so many different therapists at school and out of school. It was hard to keep track of them. Then Katani heard something strange. Did the therapist just say something about a hippo?

"Yes. Yes, I read something about hippotherapy," Mrs. Summers replied.

There it was again. Katani was sure of it! Her mother had said "hippo." Katani stood up and pressed her ear to the door. But her mother *wasn't* talking about hippos. She was saying something about horses. "I don't understand how riding a horse could be beneficial," Mrs. Summers was saying.

"It does sound odd, doesn't it?" the therapist agreed. "But I've seen hippotherapy have a dramatic effect on kids like Kelley. The rhythmic forward-and-back, side-to-side motions stimulate the rider's musculoskeletal and neural responses in the way that our equipment can't. Besides, the kids love it. For them, it's fun instead of work."

"I see," Mrs. Summers said, but Katani didn't. Katani wasn't sure exactly what this physical therapist was really talking about.

"Hippotherapy ..." the therapist said.

There was that word again.

"... is used in a variety of ways that affect the physical and psychological well-being of autistic kids. It has a calming effect. And it promotes various social and emotional benefits beyond just the physical ones."

"But is it dangerous?" Mrs. Summers asked.

"It can be a little intimidating to see your child six feet off the ground on top of a thousand pound animal, but therapeutic riding stables have a qualified staff and a large group of volunteers that run along the side of the horse. They're there not only for safety, but to provide encouragement and emotional support."

"Do you have any reading material on hippotherapy?" Mrs. Summers asked.

"Certainly," the therapist said, and Katani heard papers shuffling in the next room. "And I can recommend a nearby stable. I spoke with the owner, who specializes in working with autistic kids, this morning. She happens to have an opening. Usually there's a long waiting list. She's able to take Kelley this weekend. I suggest you give it a try."

"I don't know," Mrs. Summers hesitated. "I'd have to talk it over with my husband and my mother."

Katani glanced at her watch once again. She hoped her mother and the therapist wrapped things up quickly, the festival and the BSG were waiting for her. Hippotherapy, or whatever it was, was *not* what she wanted to be thinking about this morning!

CHAPTER 4

∞

THE GREAT ESCAPE

KATANI AND HER SISTER were two blocks away from the festival, but they could already hear the music of the carnival rides and gleeful screams from the riders. Katani could feel Kelley tensing up.

"It's OK, Kelley," Katani reassured her. "We're going to have fun. Right?"

"A ton of fun for us. Not them," Kelley said in her TV announcer voice.

Katani was amazed at how Kelley could mimic the voices she heard on TV.

"Look Katani! There's Isabel and Charlotte! This *will* be fun," Kelley shouted.

Katani looked to where Kelley was pointing. Isabel and Charlotte were standing near the carousel.

"Isabel! Charlotte!" Kelley shouted as they got close. She gave them each a big hug. Kelley wasn't always comfortable with physical contact, but when she wanted to give someone a hug, they were getting a hug—whether they liked it or not!

"Hi! Where are Avery and Maeve?" Katani asked, looking

around to see if the other BSG were nearby.

"Avery and Maeve went over to the batting cages. They both went gaga over some Red Sox player who's supposed to be there," Charlotte said.

"But for different reasons," Isabel added with a smile.

"Come on, we were just going over there. I want to check up on Marty." Charlotte began walking toward the cages.

"Marty? Marty's here? I love that little doggie! Where is he? Marty? MARTY!" Kelley shouted.

"Chill," Katani reminded Kelley. Katani was trying her best to be patient, knowing that if she got upset, Kelley would get upset as well and that would be a disaster. "We're headed that way now."

Katani didn't understand how someone so sensitive to loud noises could be so—well—LOUD!

Just over the rise on the edge of the park they could see the top of the batting cages and they hurried off in that direction. Each pitching machine whirred loudly as it spat a ball at the poised batter. If the batter connected, the ball reversed its flight with a satisfying PING! If the batter missed, the ball rattled against the cage's chain link fence backwall when it hit.

There was a small crowd gathered around the back of the batting cage and onlookers shouted out encouragement.

"You got a piece of that one!"

"Hang in there!"

"Keep your eye on the ball."

"Step into it! Step into it!"

The BSG arrived at the batting cage as the pitching machine cranked and spit out another ball. To Charlotte, it seemed that Avery swung her bat the moment the ball came out of the machine … but still, she missed the pitch.

"Wow! That was so fast! I can barely see the ball. How fast was that?" Charlotte asked.

Isabel pointed to the digital display attached to the side of the batting cage.

"Seventy-five? Seventy-five miles per hour?" Charlotte asked incredulously.

"Avery was right. This is like major league or something," Katani said. "Seriously."

"Big League," Kelley repeated with the same serious face and nod of the head. "Big League," Kelley said again just as Avery smacked a line drive back toward the pitching machine.

"WOOOOO! WHOOOOOO!!!!!" Avery shouted, dropping her bat and jumping up and down.

"Nice job, kid," said the man behind the fence.

The friendly crowd surrounding the batting cage gave her a smattering of applause.

"Alright!" Avery high-fived toward a couple of the more enthusiastic onlookers.

Kelley scrunched her eyebrows together, raised her arm and yelled, "Thank you Boston!" Even Katani had to laugh. Avery and Kelley continued to jump around.

Finally Katani said to the both of them, "It's time to settle down now!"

"Did you see him?" Maeve asked, rushing up as Avery turned back to try to hit a few more balls.

"Marty?" Kelley asked. "Did I see Marty?"

"No! Robbie Flores!" Maeve said, putting a hand to her forehead and pretending to swoon.

"Who?" Katani asked.

"That baseball player, the one that Avery was going on and on about this morning. He was just here. Right here! He's soooo dreamy! I think he might still be nearby signing autographs or something," Maeve gushed, looking frantically around.

"Marty!" Kelley yelled. "Where's Marty?"

"He's around here somewhere, Kelley," Katani turned to Maeve. "Where's Marty?"

"Yeah," Charlotte asked, examining the crowd with her reporter's eye. "Where IS Marty?"

"Wait, wait! I'm not finished. Wait until you hear this— this is the best part!" Maeve protested.

"MARTY! MARTY! Where are you?" Kelley yelled.

"You have to hear the story. Robbie Flores was sitting right there on the bench under the tree and there were tons of people around. He was signing autographs, and suddenly he stops writing, looks up, and smiles right at me! I turn to see if he's looking at someone behind me, but there is no one there. He was actually *smiling* at me. ME!"

Charlotte just shook her head. "Maeve, you are a wonder."

Kelley tilted her head back and yelled out "MARTY!" at the top of her lungs again.

"Shhhh," Katani said. She tugged on Kelley's arm, but that only seemed to make her louder.

"And ...," Maeve paused dramatically, "... and then he winked. ROBBIE FLORES WINKED AT ME! *Moi.*"

Kelley threw back her head and yelled at the top of her lungs, "MARTY!"

"So much for keeping a low profile," sighed Katani.

"Don't worry about it, Katani," Charlotte reassured her friend. "We understand."

Katani gave her a grateful smile.

"Maarty!" Kelley shouted once more.

At the final scream, Marty popped his head out of Avery's sports bag with Happy Lucky Thingy sticking out of its mouth. He gave a little growl, which was muffled by the ever patient Happy Lucky Thingy.

"Marty?" Kelley asked, trying to figure out where the sound was coming from.

Marty began wiggling faster and faster until at last, he popped right out of the duffle bag, which had been lying next to the batting cage.

"Marty! There he is!" Kelley cried happily.

Marty made a beeline for the girls. Before he could reach them, a squirrel bolted across his path. In a flash, Marty turned and dashed after it.

Off and running, his little legs were a blur of motion. With Happy Lucky Thingy sticking out of both sides of his mouth, the leash bounced along behind him like an unhappy snake on a hot skillet.

"Marty?" Kelley said softly, her mind not comprehending the situation at first. "MARTY!"

Kelley's arms and legs flailed at odd angles as she took off after the great squirrel hunter. Despite her lack of style, Kelley was incredibly fast. Katani could hardly keep up with her.

Suddenly, the squirrel bounced off the trunk of a tree and changed directions. Marty paused, wondering which was the best route for his wild pursuit. His hesitation gave Kelley, who had managed to catch up with the little dude, just enough time to stamp her foot on the end of the leash. "HA!" she yelled in triumph.

She did it! Katani thought as she panted. Kelley actually caught up with Marty and nabbed him!

However, as Kelley bent down to pick up the leash, the squirrel ran down the tree and took off in a tear toward the far end of the park.

Marty reared back. In an instant, his collar slipped off.

Kelley watched helplessly as Marty snatched up Happy Lucky, ran down the hill, and disappeared into a strand of trees.

By this time, Katani had caught up with her sister and was standing by her side.

Kelley hiccupped.

"It's OK, Kelley," Katani said, not feeling at all OK herself. "You caught him. You were the first one ..."

"MARTY!" Kelley wailed. Distraught, she threw herself on the wet grass.

Kelley's sobs grew louder. Katani was super aware that people were staring. However, at this point she didn't care. Marty had run away, but it was Kelley who had almost rescued him. Katani was proud of her sister, even though her behavior looked strange to the onlookers.

Charlotte was the first of the BSG to catch up with them. "Where's Marty?" Charlotte asked.

Hearing the name made Kelley wail louder.

Maeve and Isabel rushed over to them.

"What's the matter? Is she hurt?"

"No, no ... it's OK, Kelley," Katani said, trying to soothe her sister.

"Where's Marty?" Charlotte asked again.

Maeve tried to soothe Kelley by patting her back, but Kelley shook her head back and forth, twisted away, and sobbed into the grass. Maeve pulled her hand back. "Sorry," she whispered to Katani.

"What can we do to help?" Isabel asked.

"Nothing. Go look for Marty. I need to—to take Kelley home," Katani told her friends.

"Where *is* Marty?" Charlotte asked for the third time. Why wasn't anyone answering her?

Katani pulled the leash from beneath her sister, who was

beginning to calm down. She held it up so that the empty collar swung in the breeze.

Katani glanced up at Charlotte's shocked face.

"Which way?" was all she asked.

Katani pointed to the stand of trees down the hill and near the creek, and Charlotte disappeared.

Maeve and Isabel stayed behind to help Katani calm Kelley down.

Maeve started singing Kelley's favorite song. "Happy Birthday to you ..."

Kelley shook her head, but that didn't stop Maeve, she kept right on singing. Eventually, Kelley quieted and began to sing with Maeve. They sang "Happy Birthday" for each one of the Beacon Street Girls.

"Hey, where'd you guys go?" Avery asked as she arrived at the scene. "I got another line drive. You missed it." She took a big slurp of a Sno-Cone.

Isabel put her finger to her lips and nodded toward Kelley.

"What's going on?" Avery whispered.

"Later," Isabel mouthed to Avery.

Avery shifted her weight from foot to foot. Katani just knew what Avery was going to say next. Katani waved her hand in the air and shook her head, but she couldn't stop Avery from speaking.

"Hey, does Charlotte have Marty?" Avery asked.

Instantly, Katani, Isabel, and Maeve all said, "SHHHHH!" at the same time.

Kelley shook her head at Avery. "Avery, Marty's lost. He ran after a squirrel right before our eyes." She snapped her finger and said, "You better find him or it will just be horrible."

Katani sighed. Kelley could switch on and off so fast.

Avery's eyes popped wide open. "What do you mean?"

Katani took the leash, wadded it up behind her back in small little ball so that Kelley wouldn't see it, and handed it to Maeve. She glanced down the hill. In the distance, she could hear the echoes of Charlotte calling Marty's name.

Avery dropped her Sno-Cone and looked at the faces of her friends. She couldn't quite believe what they were saying.

"I have to take Kelley home," Katani said.

"Do you need help?" Isabel asked.

"No. I think I got it. The sooner I get her out of this crowd, the better. You guys should help Charlotte."

BLAME GAME

Maeve watched Katani and Kelley disappear into the crowd.

"So what's going on?" Avery asked in a trembling voice.

"Marty is ..." Isabel said sharply.

"What happened?" Avery's knees began to shake.

Charlotte came running back. Even though she tried to look composed, Maeve could see where tears had left streaks on her face. "Is Kelley all right?" she asked, still panting.

"Will someone please tell me what happened?" Avery pleaded.

Maeve sucked in her breath, wondering who was going to tell Avery. She twisted the leash nervously behind her back.

Charlotte grabbed the leash from Maeve's hand and held it up. "This is what happened!" she yelled.

Avery gasped. "Is that ... Marty's? How? ... When? ..." Avery was scared. She had never seen Charlotte so worked up.

"Gee ... maybe it happened while *someone* was in the batting cage," Charlotte spat out.

"But Marty was ... in my bag ... I was sure he'd be OK ... He's been fine in there before."

"Marty is an escape artist! You know that! I know that! We ALL know that!" Charlotte said, looking around at Isabel and Maeve before turning back to glare at Avery.

Tears had started to appear in Charlotte's eyes.

Maeve was shocked by Charlotte's outburst. She'd never heard Charlotte raise her voice at anyone before.

"I've already lost my poor kitty cat, Orangina, because of those boys who let him loose in the streets of Paris, and now ... I've lost ... we've lost Marty!" Charlotte sobbed, burying her face in Isabel's shoulder.

Avery bit her lip. "Which way did he go? Did you call him? Did you offer him his favorite treat? Did you whistle?"

"Wooooo whooooo! Look at me! I can hit major league pitches!" Charlotte mimicked Avery's victory dance in the batting cage. "Of course, I whistled, I yelled, and I crawled in the bushes!!"

Avery looked down at her feet.

"Charlotte, yelling at Avery isn't going to help," Maeve said firmly, as she put her hand on Charlotte's arm.

Charlotte spun around to face her. "How can she imply that I didn't do a good job looking for him when she's the one that got him lost in the first place?" Charlotte asked. Then she faced Avery. "For your information, Miss Major League Hitter, he's gone. G-O-N-E! And he doesn't have his collar on ... so even if someone does find him, they won't be able to call. They won't know who to return him to! There's no hope."

Avery's lip trembled, but she looked determined. "Well, we can't just stand here and yell at each other. Let's do something about it!"

"I WAS doing something about it. But, it's just no use. He's gone!"

Isabel looked at Maeve and bit her lip. "Charlotte ... why

don't we go home to make some fliers. If you type up the copy, I can design it," Isabel offered. Charlotte couldn't answer. Her shoulders were slumped and she couldn't look at Avery.

Maeve nodded at this suggestion. "Great idea, Isabel," she said with enthusiasm. "Something positive to focus on."

"Come on Charlotte, if we make the fliers now, we can still hand them out to people at the celebration. The sooner, the better," Isabel said. She turned back and looked at Maeve. With her eyes she looked and nodded toward Avery. Maeve was sure she knew exactly what Isabel was saying without saying a word … *you handle Avery; I'll take care of Charlotte.*

"Do you want me to help?" Avery asked timidly.

"I think you have done enough," Charlotte snapped.

Avery looked deflated as she watched Isabel and Charlotte walk away. Charlotte never got mad at anybody; Avery felt really terrible. What had started off as an incredible day was now a nightmare.

"Do you know what direction he went?" Avery asked with a sniff.

Maeve put her arm around Avery, who seemed to be shrinking smaller and smaller. "Katani saw him run down the hill and into the woods near the creek," Maeve told her.

Avery blinked back a tear, sucked in a ragged breath, and started off in that direction.

"I'll go with you," Maeve offered.

Avery shook her head. "I think you should help the others with the flier," she said.

"Come on, Avery," Maeve said, grabbing her hand. "Don't go there. Charlotte's just upset. It's not your fault. There was a squirrel. She didn't tell you that. And Kelley … you know how much Kelley loves that dog. She ran after him and then Marty got all wound up. It wasn't your fault, Avery.

❁

Really, it wasn't."

"I just hate to think of poor little Marty off all alone in the woods somewhere," Avery said. "Like all those lost pets from the hurricanes."

"He isn't all alone," Maeve reassured her. "He has Happy Lucky Thingy with him."

CHAPTER 5

ᚯ

IN SEARCH OF THE
GREAT SQUIRREL HUNTER

ISABEL SAT DOWN on the compass rose that she had drawn in the Tower and motioned for Charlotte to sit down as well. Since there were only four window seats and five BSG, this canvas floor cover was Isabel's special Tower space. Charlotte tried to steady her jumbled nerves.

Charlotte and her father had traveled the world. She'd lived on four different continents after her mother died and seen some pretty amazing things. But of all the places in the world she had visited, it was in Brookline, in the middle of the Tower, which felt the most like home.

Twirling a piece of her long honey blonde hair, Charlotte reminisced about the many slumber parties the Beacon Street Girls had enjoyed in the Tower. Marty had always added to the fun by doing all sorts of crazy things, like attacking Maeve's pink fuzzy slippers or pouncing on pieces of pizza crusts. She couldn't imagine what life would be like without Marty.

Both girls stared at the compass on the floor. It seemed to say that from this spot there were many different ways to look at things. Many different directions one could choose to go.

✿

Charlotte held a clipboard on her lap, trying to think of the perfect words to describe Marty.

"What if ..." Charlotte didn't want to say the unthinkable, but she couldn't help it. "What if we never find Marty?"

Isabel put her hand on Charlotte's arm. "You concentrate on the words. I'll sketch a design."

Charlotte nodded. She closed her eyes and Ms. Rodriguez' words came back to her. "Details! Telling details is what will make your writing come alive."

Yes, Charlotte thought. *Ms. R was right.*

Charlotte shut her eyes and waited until she saw the image of Marty in her head. He was a mutt. That didn't help. What had they decided? That he was probably terrier and something else that no one could figure out. Gray with large, dark brown eyes. Last seen in the park headed toward the creek with his favorite chew toy, Happy Lucky Thingy.

She needed an emotional tug here. She made a list.

- *Beloved pet*
- *Wiggly, cute bundle of energy.*
- *Small dog, big attitude.*
- *Answers to the name Marty or "Little Dude"*

"You finish up the sketch and I'll see if I can get this all on one page," Charlotte called over her shoulder as she disappeared through the trapdoor of the Tower and down the ladder.

After booting up her computer, she chose a bold font and somehow managed to get all the information on one page.

Isabel joined her about fifteen minutes later. Not only had she sketched an adorable picture of Marty, but she had caricatures of the five girls frowning at the bottom of the page.

"How strange," Charlotte commented as she gazed at Isabel's drawing. "Just this morning Maeve was wishing she had a caricature of herself."

"I don't think that's exactly what she had in mind," Isabel surmised.

Mr. Ramsey arrived home just as they were ready to print out lots of copies.

"Let's let my dad look at it first," suggested Charlotte.

"What's this?" Mr. Ramsey asked, looking at the flier. "Oh, no! When did this happen?"

Opening her mouth, Charlotte attempted to tell her father what happened, but tears flooded her eyes and she couldn't seem to get anything but a slight whimper out. Isabel quickly explained the whole story.

Suddenly, it was all sounding like an accident. Isabel forgot to mention how this was all Avery's fault or how Charlotte searched for Marty by crawling through the prickly scrub along the creek bed.

Charlotte wanted to tell her father the rest of the story, the real story, but when she tried to speak, nothing came out. Mr. Ramsey put his arms around his daughter.

"We have to get going," Isabel said. "I'm sorry, Mr. Ramsey. I know Charlotte's really upset, but we need to get these fliers on the street. The sooner we do, the sooner we might find Marty."

"Just a minute, Isabel," Mr. Ramsey said. "Charlotte needs to calm down before she goes anywhere. I want you to sit down and take a few deep breaths." Mr. Ramsey left to get Charlotte a big glass of cold water.

As she took the glass from her dad, her hands shook. She gulped down a nice cold sip, wondering for a second if Marty was thirsty. She thought of all the puddles around and worried that he might drink something that could make him sick. What if he was sick? What if he was really sick and helpless somewhere out there in the woods, or in a dark, scary alley all alone?

"Charlotte ... let's focus on the problem at hand," Mr. Ramsey said.

"Marty being lost?"

"Not exactly."

Mr. Ramsey stroked his chin as he gazed at the flier. "The important thing is that people get a good look at Marty. And as delightful as your illustrations of five sad Beacon Street Girls are, Isabel, it might be a little distracting."

Charlotte was afraid her father had hurt Isabel's feelings, but when she glanced at Isabel, she saw she was nodding as if what he had said made perfect sense.

"Secondly," Mr. Ramsey said, "It's not safe to put your phone number or email address on the flier. Also, why don't we scan in Marty's photo? That will really command attention. How about grabbing that photo of Marty over there on the fridge?"

"But Dad, how will—"

"Let me finish ... I can create a website where you can gather information. We can call it ... let's see ... how about www.wheresmarty.com?" he asked.

The girls looked at each other with excitement. A *Where's Marty* website. Charlotte gave her father a big hug.

While Mr. Ramsey checked to make sure no one owned the web address, Charlotte focused on the flier in front of her, crossing out the cartoon faces as well as the phone number and email address. She was already starting to catch her breath and with a sip of cold water every now and then, she was beginning to think a bit more clearly, too.

"Dad?" she asked in a steadier voice. "Do you think we should offer some sort of reward? Maybe that would make someone give Marty back."

"I think a modest reward might be a good idea," he said after some thought.

Charlotte wrote "REWARD" at the very top of the page and held her pen, waiting for the dollar amount.

"How about a hundred dollars?" he asked.

Charlotte nodded. It was more than she expected. More than she hoped for.

The girls disappeared into Charlotte's room and quickly made the changes.

They gave the flier to Mr. Ramsey for final approval. He quickly gave thumbs-up. "This looks great, girls. Why don't you take it down to Print and Copy? I'll buy the web address and start building the site."

"We can get more for our money at the Copy Cafe on Beacon Street," Charlotte said.

"We'll need strong pushpins," Isabel thought out loud. "And staplers too."

Mr. Ramsey gathered up a few rolls of tape, put some pushpins in a Baggie, and grabbed a stapler from his office. "Maybe Miss Pierce can loan you another stapler."

Charlotte and Isabel ran downstairs and knocked on the door that led to Miss Pierce's apartment. Their landlady, the reclusive Miss Pierce, opened the door.

"May I borrow a stapler?" Charlotte asked.

"Well, of course you may, Charlotte," the mysterious little woman answered. "My dear, is there anything wrong?" Miss Pierce inquired.

Charlotte had a difficult time telling the story, or even thinking about Marty lost anymore. She just wanted to hang fliers. She needed to do something. Thankfully, Isabel explained the whole situation.

"Oh, my!" exclaimed Miss Pierce, placing her hand on top of Charlotte's. "I will program my telescope to take pictures of Brookline. If Marty is running loose we will spot him." Miss Pierce was a retired astronomer and had a telescope on top of the Tower.

"Thank you so much," Isabel and Charlotte said in unison as Miss Pierce turned to get a stapler for the girls.

Charlotte was grateful that everyone was being so helpful. She hoped that all of their efforts would bring Marty home—safe and sound. Right now, the only thing that mattered to her was finding Marty.

Have You Seen ...

"We better hurry. It's getting dark more quickly these days," Isabel said as she put on her coat. "After we go to the Copy Cafe, we can split up from there."

Charlotte just nodded as she threw on her coat. She still felt angry. Isabel had made it seem like losing Marty had all been an unavoidable accident when she told her father and Miss Pierce what had happened. Why hadn't Isabel mentioned that Avery was supposed to be watching Marty? Why was everyone being so protective of someone who says they love dogs but wasn't paying attention? It hadn't been an accident at all. It had happened because Avery was more interested in the batting cage than taking care of Marty. And now Marty might be lost forever ... just like Orangina, her poor kitty cat that she had left behind in Paris. The thought burned Charlotte up inside. The yellow Victorian wouldn't be the same without Marty—nor would the Beacon Street Girls. She wiped a tear out of the corner of her eye.

Isabel walked silently beside Charlotte as they hurried toward downtown.

As they headed out into the sunny afternoon, all Charlotte could think about were the pictures and TV images of the lost animals from Hurricane Katrina. She felt a pang of panic. What if they couldn't find Marty?

"How many copies?" the clerk at Copy Cafe asked when they handed him the flier.

"I have a five," Isabel said.

"I have a ten," Charlotte said. "Can we get as many copies as fifteen dollars will buy? That should be enough to get started."

When Charlotte had stuffed the ten dollar bill in her pocket this morning, she'd thought about buying a new T-shirt or perhaps a new bracelet. The day had turned out much differently.

"Well girls," the man took out a calculator. "At 10 cents a copy that's 150 fliers! You must be serious about finding this little dog!"

When the print job was completed, they divided the fliers between them. "You take Harvard and I will take Beacon," an in-charge Isabel directed. She could tell that her friend Charlotte was worried and confused.

"I'll meet you back at the corner."

Charlotte's first stop was Irving's.

"Twice? How very nice," Mrs. Weiss said, laughing at her little rhyme. "Did you fill up the reporter's book already?"

"Not exactly ..." Charlotte said. "We have an emergency."

Charlotte showed Mrs. Weiss the flier. "Do you think that we could tape this in your front window and maybe right here by the counter?"

Mrs. Weiss took the flier from Charlotte's hand and read

the whole thing.

"Oh, my goodness," she said, clutching the front of her floral dress. "Little Marty lost? Oh, my dear, you must feel awful. You had him on a leash, how in heaven's name did he get away from you?"

"He didn't get away from me ..." Charlotte said, tersely. "He got away from Avery."

"Oh?" Mrs. Weiss turned her head to one side, encouraging Charlotte to continue.

"Yes. She left him in her duffle bag while she was at the batting cage." Charlotte sniffled. "If she hadn't been so interested in having a good time, Marty would be home with me right now," she said.

"You know, Charlotte, everyone gets distracted sometimes. I mean, here we are having a big festival and there are rides and games and cotton candy. And that little Avery, when she comes in here she bounces around like she's one of those Superballs over there. A regular little Superball."

For a moment, Charlotte caught herself smiling at the image of Avery bouncing about like a ball. Then she got mad again. She knew that Mrs. Weiss was right, but she just couldn't stop being mad at Avery right now.

Mrs. Weiss patted Charlotte's hand. "You'll find the little doggie. And don't be so hard on the bouncy one"

"But Avery ..."

"She's a good little egg, that Avery," Mrs. Weiss interrupted. "I bet she feels as bad as you do ... or worse! She loves that dog." Charlotte nodded and waved good-bye to Mrs. Weiss. She knew the storeowner was right, but she just couldn't shake the feeling that if Avery had been more responsible, none of this would be happening. They would all be at the festival eating hot dogs and munching on popcorn.

Every time Charlotte entered a shop, she asked permission to tape up her sign. By the time she was done, there was a Marty flier plastered in every store window on Harvard Street. Marty would be famous. Charlotte thought the little dude would be pleased.

When Charlotte met up with Isabel at the end of the street, she was feeling more hopeful. Surely somebody would have seen the little dude by now.

"Any luck?" Isabel asked.

Charlotte shook her head. "You?" she asked.

Isabel shook her head.

As they walked back into the park, they noticed the vendors starting to put away their wares for the day and the crowd beginning to thin out.

The girls wished each other luck and then trudged off separately into the remains of the fair.

"Have you seen this dog?" Charlotte asked each vendor, holding up the sign.

"No," was the universal reply.

Most people said they would keep their eyes open, but some didn't even want to take the flier. With every step Charlotte took, fear grew in her heart that she might never see Marty again.

When she got to the end of the first row of vendors, Charlotte spotted Avery's jacket folded into a lump and abandoned at the base of the big tree in the park. *I can't believe it!* Charlotte thought. Avery not only lost Marty but her jacket too. But when she got to the tree she realized that the jacket was not alone. There was Avery, all curled up into such a tight, tiny ball that Charlotte had almost missed her.

"Avery?" Charlotte asked.

Avery looked up. Her eyes were swollen and red—her

✿

cheeks streaked with tears. She looked so small and lost that Charlotte instantly felt sorry for her.

"I looked and looked and looked," said Avery, standing up. Her legs were streaked with mud and scratched from crawling through the bushes. "I kept calling him and I whistled so long and hard," Avery said with a hoarse voice. Charlotte knew that she was telling her the truth, but she still couldn't help thinking that Avery was the one who got into this mess in the first place. At the same time, she felt sorry for Avery. It was all so confusing.

"Don't act like the Lone Ranger. You're not the only one who's been looking."

Avery gulped. "I know you're mad, Charlotte, but what else do you want me to do?"

Charlotte felt instantly guilty for what she'd said. *But it was all true*, Charlotte reminded herself. Marty wouldn't be missing if Avery hadn't been thinking of herself and baseball!

Then she remembered what Mrs. Weiss had said about not focusing on blame, but focusing on finding Marty instead.

"Come on," Charlotte said, and offered her hand to Avery, pulling her to her feet. "Take a few fliers. It's getting late. This has been a hard day for me, and I think I took it out on you." That was as close as Charlotte could get to an apology. She knew she had been beastly, but losing Marty had made her feel so sad.

CR

"What's up Ave—did you ...?" Isabel asked when they met up at the end of the section of vendors.

Avery shook her head.

Isabel gave Avery a hug. "Are you OK? You look awful."

"I'm better now, actually," said Avery. She wiped off her

cheeks and jumped up and down to regroup. An anxious Charlotte was suddenly reminded of the super bouncy ball in Mrs. Weiss's store.

"What's next?" Avery asked. "We gotta DO something!"

"Maybe we could call the TV stations. The radio stations. The more people who know, the better," Isabel suggested.

"That's a great idea," Avery said enthusiastically.

Charlotte wasn't so sure. "Why would the TV stations care about a little lost dog? Boston must have much more exciting things going on than that."

"Have you got a better suggestion?" Isabel asked with a tinge of annoyance in her voice.

Charlotte looked at Isabel and Avery. She had to admit that she was out of options. Calling the radio and TV stations was better than nothing.

"Come on, we can call from my house," she said.

And the three girls walked dejectedly up the hill toward Charlotte's house.

CHAPTER 6

❧

NEIGH!

SUNDAY NIGHT Katani started her favorite routine—laying out her clothes for school the next day—when her mother called her from the other room.

"Katani, could you come into the living room for a minute? Your father and I would like to talk to you."

Uh-oh, the living room. This must be serious, she reasoned. The living room was only reserved for special occasions in the Summers household. But Katani couldn't imagine what was so important to discuss on a Sunday night just before bedtime. Nevertheless, she quickly folded up her jeans, laid them on the bed, and went to join her parents.

"In here," Mrs. Summers said, motioning her into the small office off the living room. When Katani stepped in, her mother shut the door behind them both and sat next to her father on the small loveseat. She motioned for Katani to sit in the desk chair. What could this be about? Her parents looked so nervous. She knew that she hadn't done anything wrong. Her heart gave a leap. She hoped they weren't going to tell her that something terrible had happened to Marty.

Katani leaned forward.

"Marty—something terrible happened …?"

"No, no, honey," her mother rushed to reassure her. "We haven't heard anything." Seeing the concern on her daughter's face she added, "I am sure little Marty will be found. Your dad says the fliers are all over town."

Katani heaved a sigh of relief and leaned back in her chair.

"So what do you want then? I hope it's not more babysitting," said Katani, folding her arms across her chest.

Her mother gave her the look that said, "No sass from you young lady." Katani sat up straight in her chair and listened up.

"Katani, I don't know how much you overheard at the physical therapist's office the other day," began Mrs. Summers.

Katani gulped. Was she in trouble for eavesdropping? "Not much," she stammered.

"Perhaps you overheard us talking about hippotherapy?" Mrs. Summers asked.

There was that word again.

Katani nodded. But a sudden stab of fear struck. Was something wrong with Kelley? Something serious?

"What does it mean?" she asked in a soft voice. "I know it doesn't have to do with hippopotamuses."

Mr. Summers' lips crept into a smile.

"No, Ms. Know Everything. It's horseback riding therapy. *Hippo* is the Latin word for horse. Hippopotamus actually means *water horse*," he explained.

"Oh," Katani answered, relieved. She couldn't wait to somehow bring this up in front of Charlotte. The *word nerd* would be very impressed with her.

"We called the stable that the physical therapist recommended—the High Hopes Riding Stable," her mother said." "They have an immediate opening and can accept Kelley right away."

Katani looked up at the hopeful tone in her mother's voice. "That's great," Katani said, still wondering what all this had to do with her.

Her parents looked at each other.

"Well, Katani," her father started. "Horse riding therapy helps improve many, many aspects of autistic kids' lives. We feel very lucky to have found a stable that has a therapeutic riding program for autistic kids—one that had an opening."

"Uh-huh," Katani nodded, becoming suspicious. She knew her parents didn't call her into the room to describe her sister's therapy.

"Well," her mother continued. "Claudia McClelland, the director at the stable, says it helps if the autistic child has a peer role model …"

The term "peer role model" set off alarms in Katani's head. She'd heard this term before, many times before. It meant they liked to have a "normal kid" to cue Kelley on how to behave. Someone Kelley was familiar with, and someone close to her age. Usually, that meant Katani.

Mrs. Summers kept on, but Katani had zoned out. The idea of climbing on top of a 1,000-pound animal wasn't her cup of tea. She just wanted to go back to her room and plan her outfit for tomorrow.

"… So what do you think?" her mother asked.

"Think about what?"

"About accompanying your sister to therapeutic horseback riding lessons?"

"You mean like walking her there, like I took her to the physical therapist?" Katani asked, wondering how far away this place was. There weren't any riding stables within walking distance that she knew of.

"No, your grandmother will be driving you to the riding stable." Her mother was starting to look exasperated.

"So why do I have to go?"

Her mother sighed.

"Ms. McClelland says it's easier for autistic children if they have a peer role model."

There was that word again.

"Me? I'm supposed to be her peer role model?"

"Yes."

"What do I have to do?"

Her parents made eye contact again.

"Katani, you'd be taking riding lessons as well," her father explained.

"What! No! I'm scared of horses. They're enormous. I don't like this idea at all!!"

"Neither does Kelley, but it would be so much easier for her if …"

"Easier for her? What about me! Does anyone ever think about what I might like to do? How I might like to spend my free time?"

"Katani …" her mother started.

"No way! Mom, I have enough to worry about with school and all the things I want to do. And now Marty is lost and I have to help. Can't Patrice do it?"

"Patrice is in high school with an intense work load and she has basketball practice every day. And you know that we are hoping for an athletic scholarship for her."

"Well … can't you find someone else?"

"Katani," her mother tried to sound optimistic, "Look on the bright side. This could be fun for you."

"Fun? When have I ever given you the idea that sitting on

top of some old horse was my idea of fun? I don't want to."

"Well … Katani," her father said in a strained voice. "We were hoping that you'd want to. But, the fact is that everything has already been arranged."

"What? My opinion doesn't even count? You have got to be kidding me. That's so unfair."

"Katani …"

Her mother tried to describe the benefits and how important having a peer role model would be, but Katani was no longer listening.

She scrunched down in the chair.

"You didn't even ask me first. This is so typical."

Her father took a deep breath. He was a large man and when he breathed in deeply he seemed to double in size.

"Katani," he said in an exasperated voice. "This is what being in a family means—making sacrifices for the people you love. Your mom and I love you as much as Kelley, Patrice, and Candice. But we have to balance everyone's needs. I know it might not seem fair right now, but things balance out in the end. No one asked Kelley if she wanted to be autistic. But she is, and we all have to deal with it."

Mrs. Summers closed the argument. "Being in a family with an autistic sister requires that you pitch in, that you do what you can. We've all made sacrifices for Kelley."

Katani was silent. She knew deep down her parents were right. She remembered the summer when her sister's friends went to camp, and Patrice had to stay home and baby-sit Katani and Kelley.

"Your first lesson is tomorrow afternoon." Her father got up, patted her on the shoulder, and left the room.

Katani didn't move.

Mrs. Summers sat quietly with Katani for a while. "I

hope that you'll see this is an opportunity for you as well."

Katani shrugged and swirled the desk chair so her back was facing her mother. Mrs. Summers got up and leaned over to kiss her daughter on her cheek and left the room.

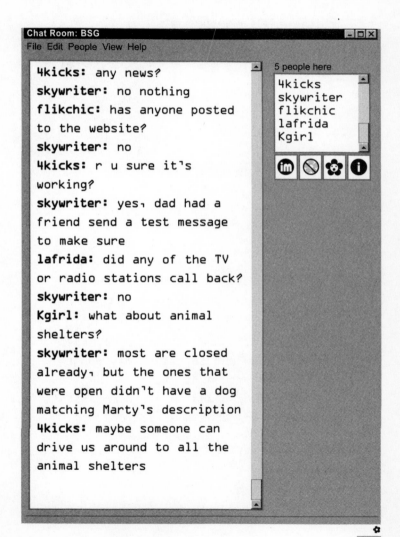

4kicks: any news?

skywriter: no nothing

flikchic: has anyone posted to the website?

skywriter: no

4kicks: r u sure it's working?

skywriter: yes, dad had a friend send a test message to make sure

lafrida: did any of the TV or radio stations call back?

skywriter: no

Kgirl: what about animal shelters?

skywriter: most are closed already, but the ones that were open didn't have a dog matching Marty's description

4kicks: maybe someone can drive us around to all the animal shelters

Chat Room: BSG

File Edit People View Help

5 people here

4kicks
skywriter
flikchic
lafrida
Kgirl

File Edit People View Help

skywriter: who? When? Dad has office hours tomorrow evening
flikchic: we'll put our heads together. we'll figure something out

5 people here

4kicks
skywriter
flikchic
lafrida
Kgirl

To: Sophie
From: Charlotte
Subject: Marty

sophie-

marty's lost! if someone does find him, they won't know who to call. they don't know where to return him to!
it's like losing orangina all over again!
i'm heartbroken. What should I do?
Ton amie,
charlotte

Avery's Blog

Friends, family, countrymen, I need your help!

The BSG's adorable, lovable little dog has run away!

Last seen running toward the creek at the Brookline 300 Festival on Saturday afternoon. He's not wearing a collar, but answers to Marty.

Email me if you have any leads!

CHAPTER 7

❧

RHYME TIME

AVERY WAS THE LAST ONE through the door to English class when the bell rang.

Ms. Rodriguez had poems pinned up all over the room. Some of the poems were funny and some were kind of sad or confusing, especially the ones by poets who lived a long time ago. Some, in Avery's opinion, were kind of ridiculous. They didn't make any sense to her at all.

Every teacher since third grade had taught a poetry unit, which Avery usually hated. She had to admit that Ms. R had made her think about poetry in a different way. She said that it didn't have to rhyme. That poetry could be about emotions and passion or a cause important to the writer. And to think of poetry as a puzzle. What was the writer trying to say? The hints were in the words and images. Ms. R described poems as a wonderful dessert, rich and sweet, full of flavors to nourish the soul. Avery liked the dessert analogy, but she still would rather eat a cupcake than read poetry—no offense to Ms. R.

Avery had struggled with the weekend homework assignment. They were supposed to write a poem ...

something they were passionate about.

At first, Avery considered writing her poem about losing Marty. But she was afraid that if Ms. Rodriguez asked her to read the poem out loud, she might cry. It was bad enough that she had cried at the festival on Saturday. Good thing none of the guys, especially Billy Trentini, had seen her blubbering like a baby over a lost dog. So she decided to pick another topic.

Avery had stayed up late last night working on her poem. She thought long and hard. What was she passionate about? Just as she was about to freak out and say she couldn't possibly do this, Scott walked into her room and threw a Nerf baseball at her head.

Perfect. The light bulb went off. "Go away, Scott. I have to write a poem."

When she pulled her homework assignment out of her notebook, it was all rumpled because she had stuffed it into her bag in a rush. She began to smooth out the crinkled edges as she waited for Ms. Rodriguez to start class.

"OK ... class, settle down," the teacher said. "How many of you went to the festival this weekend?"

Avery looked around. It seemed everyone's hands shot up in the air. Usually her hand would have been the first up, but because of what happened with Marty, she didn't raise hers.

"Well, I hope you all found time to work on your poems between the rides and games," Ms. R said with a smile. Then she surveyed the room, making sure that her students had done their assignments.

"I have a poem that I love. It's about spring, but I remember it made me think of the festival because of all the balloons in the park. It's called 'In Just' by e. e. cummings."

Ms. Rodriguez walked up and down the aisles as she read the poem.

"in Just-
spring when the world is mud-
luscious ..."

Avery sighed as Ms. R read the rest of the poem. That poem was OK, but what was with those old words like *"far and wee"*? They sounded so weird.

"Over the weekend you were asked to write a poem about something you are passionate about," Ms. Rodriguez said.

Avery squirmed in her seat.

There were lots of sighs heard from around the class.

Dillon looked at Avery and rolled his eyes. Avery wanted to laugh, but she was afraid Ms. Rodriguez would see her.

Betsy Fitzgerald raised her hand. "I'd like to share my poem with the class, Ms. R."

Now it was Avery's turn to roll her eyes. *A poem by Betsy. Oh, boy, this was going to be good.* Avery could hardly wait.

"Let me guess," she whispered to Pete Wexler, who was sitting right next to her. "Betsy's probably passionate about how she color-coded the paperclips in her desk drawer."

Pete squelched a laugh, which made it look and sound like a loud sneeze instead. Ms. Rodriguez glared at them both. Avery flashed her very best I'm-paying-attention-and-can't-wait-to-hear-Betsy's-poem smile.

Ms. Rodriguez raised her eyebrows ... Avery knew she was skating on thin ice. She'd have to try extra hard to show fake enthusiasm for Betsy's poetry.

Betsy Fitzgerald stood up and went to the front of the room. She cleared her throat, took a deep breath, and began ... *"Perseverance."*

She paused and looked proudly around the room. Avery figured Betsy thought the title alone was impressive enough for applause.

Avery couldn't resist: "Perseverance? That's what she's passionate about?" she said out of the side of her mouth. Pete didn't make a sound, but he began shaking all over.

Betsy's poem had a lot of big words and rhymed like she was reading something from Mother Goose. Now sometimes, thought Avery, Mother Goose is funny. But there was nothing funny about Betsy's poem. It was boring with a capital B and really serious. And she read like she was on stage doing Shakespeare, pausing dramatically after every line, as if to give the class time to understand her *deep ideas*. Avery couldn't help yawning and putting her head down on the desk. The poem seemed to drone on forever. It's too bad Betsy didn't have a cape and a sword, thought Avery. That might improve her performance.

By the time Betsy finished, Avery was afraid to turn around. What if everyone in the class had fallen asleep?

"Thank you for sharing, Betsy," Ms. Rodriguez said as she clapped loudly. Ms. R always made everyone clap after someone got up and presented. This time she probably wanted to wake every one up, figured Avery as she joined in. Betsy walked back to her desk nodding to her classmates.

"Perseverance is very important. I bet we have some other inspiring pieces as well," Ms. R said, looking around at the restless class.

Pete Wexler raised his hand. "I wrote about pretzels."

"Pretzels?" Maeve asked. "I can't believe that you're passionate about pretzels!"

"Yeah," Pete said, "I am." Unlike Betsy, he read his poem sitting in his desk chair.

✿

Ode to a Pretzel

My dad takes me to Fenway Park,
Where snack food vendors like to bark.

"Pizza, come on, get your cheese!"
None for me, Dad, if you please.
"Fenway Franks, here, Fenway Franks!"
Fenway Franks today? No thanks!

"Soda, soda, get your pick!"
The thought of soda makes me sick!
"Peanuts, peanuts, cashews too!"
Peanuts? Cashews? Boo, boo, boo!

When I'm in my Fenway seat
There's just one thing that I would eat.

It's warm, it's soft, it's great to chew,
It's doughy, sweet, and salty too.

When Dad takes me to Fenway Park
And snack food vendors start to bark

There's only one that makes me cheer:
"Pretzels—get your pretzels, here!"

No matter if it's rain or shine
A pretzel will make the game fine.

So if the Sox (gasp) LOSE the game
The pretzels make me glad I came.

Avery thought it was pretty funny, and so did the rest of the class. Ms. R called it "simply marvelous." Pete blushed big time. Avery didn't think anyone had ever complimented Pete Wexler on his schoolwork before. He was probably in shock. Avery was getting excited now. If what the class wanted was chuckles, wait until they heard her poem.

"Thank you, Peter. You sound very moved about pretzels, you sound …"

"I was. I got a humongous pretzel at the Sox game. Dillon and I went to Fenway on Saturday."

"Awesome game," Joey Peppertone blurted out. "I saw it on TV."

"What happened?" Avery asked. She was usually the resident expert on the Red Sox, but she'd been so exhausted and upset from worrying about Marty that she'd only quickly checked the score a couple of times. Between Marty and having to write a poem, Avery had abandoned her beloved baseball team. She felt like a totally disloyal fan.

"Will someone please tell me?" she looked frantically around the room.

"Where were you? On the moon?" Dillon asked. "Flores broke out of his hitting slump on Saturday night."

"He did?"

"Yup. A single, a double, and a three-run homer. Six RBIs in all."

"Woooo HOOOO!" Avery shouted as she leapt up from her seat.

"Avery!" Ms. Rodriguez said, giving her a stern look. "Keep it down."

"I'm sorry, Ms. R. It's just that Robbie Flores is what I'm passionate about."

"Me, too," Maeve sighed.

"I even wrote my poem about him," said Avery.

"Would you like to share it with the class?" Ms. Rodriguez asked.

"Yeah!"

Avery popped out of her chair and rushed to the front of the room then spun around to face the class. She was so excited about Robbie Flores that she just knew the class, especially the Red Sox fans, would love her poem.

The poem was short. AND it could be acted out—at least a little. As Avery read her poem, she swung an imaginary bat and jumped up in the air, pretending to catch a fly ball in the outfield.

Rookie of the Year

Extra! Extra! Read all about it!
Red Sox are gonna win, no doubt about it!

Forget about Babe Ruth and move back Sosa
Our dude makes Mark McGuire look like a posa

Sorry, Ms. Rodriguez, but I'd rather play some hookie,
I want to go to Fenway NOW to see the brand new rookie!

His name is Robbie Flores, and some girls say he's cute,
But I just care cause he's the best *new ballplayer to BOOT!*

Curve ball, fast ball, leftie pitch or right
It doesn't even matter—Flores hits it out of sight.

Extra! Extra! Flores gets it done!
He's up at bat again and hits another sweet home run!

When Robbie Flores stands at bat he looks so strong and brave
The sight of him alone will make the Sox fans do a "wave."

"Boo Yankees! Boo Yankees!" some fans like to cheer.
But I will shout, "Go, Flores! You're the rookie of the year!"

So if you bring your mitt for catching Flores' pop fly,
Please don't hold your breath or get your little hopes too high.

Chances are if Robbie takes a swing at any ball,
The only thing to catch it will be the old Green Monster wall!

Extra! Extra! To the World Series, we are bound!
I wonder what good luck it is that Robbie Flores found.

I was great, Avery thought smugly as the class clapped
and whistled. Avery smiled and took a bow. Pete and Dillon
stomped their feet for emphasis. Avery was probably the
only girl in the whole school who could get away with a
performance like that, laughed Maeve.

"Enough," Ms. Rodriguez said between laughs. "Avery
obviously has a lot of passion for baseball, the Red Sox, and
especially Robbie Flores in particular. Thank you for sharing,
Avery. You can go back to your seat now."

On her way back to her seat, Avery high-fived Maeve
and Dillon.

BACK TO REALITY

Charlotte felt sick to her stomach as Avery read her
poem. How could she be so happy and carefree when Marty
was lost somewhere? And to top it off, Avery's poem was
about baseball, reminding Charlotte what had started this

whole mess. It's a good thing she sat on the other side of the room. She was so distraught that she didn't want to be near Avery right now.

"Can I go next?" Charlotte asked when the noise finally died down. Charlotte stood at the front of the room. She read her poem about losing Marty.

A Rhyme for Marty

Losing a pet is like losing a best friend,
No comforting words can anyone send.
I hope Marty's safe, not scared and alone.
More than anything, I want Marty to come back home.

If he doesn't, it will never ever be the same.
Nothing will make it better, not wealth or fame.
If Marty the dog is gone forever,
Sunny days will seem like bad weather.

When Charlotte finished, she looked up from the paper. She looked right at Avery. Avery's head was face down on the desk.

There was no yelling or whistling. There was no laughing or stomping of feet. Everyone seemed sad and serious.

"Avery," Ms. Rodriguez said. "Are you OK?"

Avery raised her head and shook it sadly. Tears were running down her face. Ms. R grabbed some tissues and brought them to Avery.

Suddenly, Charlotte felt awful. She remembered Mrs. Weiss's advice. "Everybody gets distracted sometimes." Was she actually starting to be mean to Avery? *She's obviously as upset as I am about losing Marty, she just doesn't always show it the same way.*

"As you can see from the four poems we heard today," Ms. Rodriguez went on, "poetry can pack a big punch. Have you found little Marty, yet?"

"No," Charlotte said, her voice breaking. "WE lost him on Saturday. He's been missing for ..." Charlotte checked her watch. "For forty-five hours. We've looked everywhere. It's like he ...vanished. Into thin air. I don't know what to do."

The class was silent. Everyone knew that the BSG were crazy about their little adopted dog.

"Maybe someone kidnapped him ... you know," Joey Peppertone suggested.

Kidnapped! That had never occurred to Charlotte. She assumed that like the pets that were stranded in hurricane areas, Marty was lost out there along the creek or the Charles River. Lost and homeless. But ... *kidnapped*! She snuck a look at Avery. Her tear stained face pained Charlotte.

Dillon jumped in. "Hey ... I saw that on some TV show ... dogs were missing all over this neighborhood and ..."

"I doubt that's the case here, Dillon," Ms. Rodriguez interrupted before Dillon could reveal any more disturbing details. "Charlotte, do you have any fliers?"

Charlotte nodded.

"Perhaps we all could take a few posters and help distribute them around all the neighborhoods. Why don't you get them out, Charlotte, and anyone who would like to help can take a few," Ms. Rodriguez suggested.

Charlotte pulled the stack of fliers from her book bag and handed them to Ms. R.

"Why don't I leave them on my desk?" she asked.

At the end of the class, the BSG waited as their classmates all came up and grabbed a few fliers. Even Anna and Joline, the famous Queens of Mean, took some. Maeve exchanged surprised glances with Charlotte.

"Maybe they're not as bad as we think they are," Maeve said as Charlotte gathered the remaining fliers and left the classroom.

"Maybe they have a sweet side we don't know about," Isabel said.

Katani looked at her like she was crazy. "Yeah right! And God doesn't make little green apples and it don't rain in Indianapolis in the summer time."

"What?" Charlotte asked.

"It's a song," Maeve said. "An old song ... good one."

"What I mean is, those two were probably showing off for Ms. R. You know how they like to pretend they're sweet in front of the teachers. I bet they've wadded them up and thrown them away already," Katani said.

"No, Katani," Isabel spoke up. "I think you're wrong. They both like Marty. I ran into them into the park once and they were really nice to him. Joline even said he was 'adorable.'"

Katani wasn't so sure. She would believe it when she saw a flier in Brookline Village where they both lived.

Avery's Blog

Why Robbie Flores should be Rookie of the Year
- *Highest batting average*
- *Highest number of RBIs*
- *Highest slugging percentage*
- *More than 20 stolen bases*

Marty's still missing. Almost 48 hours gone. Where is he?

CHAPTER 8

ଓଃ

HIGH HOPES

CHARLOTTE WAS ALARMED when she arrived home with Maeve to find her father's bike on the front porch. He wasn't supposed to be back from school until after six on Mondays. Was there something ...

"Dad?" she called up the stairs as soon as she pushed through the big wooden front door of the yellow Victorian. "Are you home, Dad?"

"In here, Char," he called down from the kitchen.

Charlotte pounded up the stairs. Her father was bustling about in the kitchen. "Hello girls," he said as he stirred a pot of fragrant soup.

"What's going on Dad? Why are you here so early?"

"It's Monday. I cancelled my office hours today. I thought ... where are the rest of the BSG?" he looked over at Maeve.

"Katani had to help her sister and Isabel and Avery had basketball practice. So Maeve came with me. She said she didn't want me to come home alone to an empty Marty-less house," Charlotte sighed.

"Ah, that's nice, of you, Maeve. Well, don't leave her

standing in the foyer, Charlotte." Mr. Ramsey beckoned for Maeve to come in.

"How about some popcorn and chocolate milk, ladies?"

"Yes, please," both girls nodded. "Popcorn is a favorite in the Kaplan-Taylor home, Mr. Ramsey," added Maeve as she sat down at the kitchen table.

"Well, Maeve, I don't think my popcorn will stand up to your dad's, but for an afternoon snack it will have to do," laughed Mr. Ramsey. Everyone knew that the Brookline Movie House—the theater that Maeve's parents owned—had the best popcorn in town.

"Dad ..."

"Charlotte ..."

Both Charlotte and her father spoke at the same time.

"You first, Dad," Charlotte said as she grabbed a handful of warm, buttery popcorn.

"Listen, I thought we could spend some time this afternoon visiting animal hospitals and shelters. While I was waiting for you to get here, Charlotte, I looked up all the clinics and marked them on the map. If someone found Marty, they might have taken him to one of these places."

Charlotte got up and hugged her dad. It was so great of him to come home from work to help them search for Marty.

"Mr. Ramsey," Maeve interjected. "That is a brilliant plan. Don't you think so, Charlotte?"

"Not only do I think it's brilliant, but I think we should get going right away. And Dad ..."

Her father looked at his daughter with a reassuring smile. He knew how important finding Marty was to Charlotte.

"Can we stop at the Copy Cafe first and get more copies? Oh ... and before we leave I need to check the website," Charlotte said.

"I already checked, sweetheart."

"And ...?" Charlotte asked a twinge of hopefulness in her voice.

Mr. Ramsey shook his head. "Nothing."

Charlotte choked back a sob. She couldn't cry now. They had work to do.

Maeve looked pensive. "Mr. Ramsey ... Perhaps we could drive by the park first. Maybe Marty returned to the last place he saw us," she suggested.

Charlotte doubted that this was possible, but she was touched by Maeve's concern.

"Good idea, Maeve. Let's get going," Charlotte said, heading toward the door.

Charlotte was happy that both her father and Maeve were there to help her look for Marty, but it was Monday afternoon. Marty had already been missing for forty-eight hours. Charlotte was beginning to lose hope.

Maeve must have read the worry on Charlotte's face. "Don't worry, Char," she said, squeezing her friend's hand. "We'll never stop looking for Marty!"

HIP, HIPPO-RAY!

Katani sat next to Kelley in the middle seat of Big Blue, her grandmother's old boat-sized blue car, and stared out the window. Normally, Katani loved to go for a ride in Big Blue. Usually it meant a trip to the mall or a day trip to Cape Cod. Ruby Fields loved to take her granddaughters on little adventures. She said it was "good for the soul."

Today was different, however. They were going out to Weston to the High Hopes Therapeutic Riding Stable. Weston was a half-hour away from their home in Brookline. That meant in addition to the riding lessons, Katani had to spend an hour in the car with her sister instead of hanging out with her friends, or more importantly, looking for Marty.

Katani was really worried about Charlotte. Char was so angry with Avery and her role in Marty's disappearance that Katani was afraid it might impact their friendship. It was so unlike the normally sensitive Charlotte to get that mad or mad at all. *Perhaps*, wondered Katani as she stared out the window, *it was easier to be angry than feel sad that Marty might be lost forever*. As they got closer to the stables, they entered a semi-wooded suburban area of Boston that Katani had never been to before. It was lovely, but she wouldn't let herself admire the beautiful trees or the graceful colonial homes. She didn't want to go horseback riding—and that was that.

Meanwhile, Mrs. Fields was explaining in a calm voice to Kelley what lay ahead. "You girls are so lucky. I've never ridden a horse before," her grandmother said. "But I always wanted to. When I was your age, I had friends who rode. Oh, the stories they told. Riding on trails through the woods and going to horse shows."

Kelley clapped her hands, "Ha! I will ride a horse today."

Mrs. Fields looked fondly at both of her granddaughters.

Katani refused to respond and instead turned to stare out the window. She wasn't ready to admit how the lush green trees and stone walls appealed to her finely tuned sense of style.

When they got closer, Grandma Ruby passed the directions to Katani. Grandma Ruby was famous for getting lost, and Katani didn't feel like driving around for an extra hour or two.

Katani was relieved when she saw a small sign that read *High Hopes*. She shouted, "There it is, Grandma! Turn here."

Grandma Ruby rolled onto a country road that was

surrounded by big maple trees. On the corner was a big old shingle-styled house that looked like it was once a hotel. Just past the house was a small riding stable. As they pulled in, Kelley began to bounce up and down. There were horses in the paddock. Curious, they stuck their heads over the fence to stare at Big Blue. Katani put her fingers to her mouth to keep from smiling. She figured the horses had never seen anything like Big Blue before.

Katani had imagined a huge pasture, white fences, and lots of thoroughbred horses running around. What she saw instead was a small brown weathered barn that looked like it might blow over in the next strong wind. There was a fence, but it was brown, not white. And there wasn't an endless pasture area, just a ring with a clump of grass in the middle. The recent rain had left the area muddy, and the ruts in the driveway were filled with water. *Not the stuff of TV*, Katani thought.

"We're here!" Grandma Ruby sang out. "Come on girls."

"Ooooo!" Kelley said when she opened the door. She pinched her nose closed with her fingers.

Kelley was right. It was smelly. Katani promised herself that she would take a half-hour shower when she got home. OK, maybe an hour.

"Look Katani. Horses!" Kelley yelled, and pointed to two horses in the tiny ring. Two more horses were tied up to the side of the barn. "Just like on the carousel. I want to ride a pink-and-lavender one. Do they have a pink-and-lavender one?"

"These are real horses," Mrs. Fields explained to Kelley. "Horses are brown, and black, and white, and grey. Some even have spots."

Suddenly, one of the horses in the ring let out a big snort and stamped his foot on the ground. Kelley jumped about a foot in the air and grabbed a hold of her sister. Katani felt like jumping too. Those horses were *big*!

Mrs. Fields led her reluctant granddaughters to the fence. Something had spooked the horses and they began a slow trot around the ring, their manes flying behind them in the wind. The horse with a white splotch on its forehead held its tail high. Katani had to admit that he looked beautiful and proud. She leaned her head over the fence to get a closer look

"Oooh," Kelley exclaimed as the horses moved closer. Suddenly, the one with a splotch on its forehead stopped and reached its head over the rails. Kelley jumped back. Unafraid, Grandma Ruby stuck her flat palm out and let the horse nuzzle her.

"You are one lucky girl, Kelley. You're going to learn to ride!" Kelley looked at her grandmother with a comical face that seemed to say, "I'm not too sure about this."

"This is a great opportunity for you, too, Katani. Not everyone gets a chance to do this type of thing."

Katani knew better than to roll her eyes in front of her grandmother, but she didn't smile either.

Yeah, Katani thought. *I hope I don't ruin my jeans.*

The horse continued to paw the ground and snort. Katani wondered what that horse wanted.

"I want to go home now," Kelley said. "I don't want to ride real horses. I want to ride on the carousel."

Before Grandma Ruby could respond, a young woman walked over. She had short, curly blonde hair and big, friendly, blue eyes. She was wearing jeans, a bulky sweater, a vest, and some kind of mud boots. Katani thought she looked like an ad in a magazine.

"You must be Mrs. Summers," the woman said, offering her hand to Grandma Ruby.

"No, I'm Kelley's grandmother, Mrs. Fields," Grandma Ruby said, taking the woman's hand and shaking it.

"Nice to meet you, I'm Claudia McClelland. You must be Katani. And YOU must be Kelley. You girls can call me Claudia. So have either of you ever been on a horse before?"

This woman was all business, thought Katani, who shook her head no. She knew she was supposed to be the brave one, but she didn't feel particularly brave at the moment.

"I rode a horse at the festival. It was pink and lavender. It was pretty … so pretty," Kelley enthused.

"It was on the carousel," Katani interrupted. She didn't want Kelley to go off on a tangent about pretty pink-and-lavender horses.

Claudia nodded like she knew all about the episode last Saturday. She reached up and patted the horse's head.

"Well, I see you met Sadie here," she said as Sadie nuzzled her hair. Katani made a face. There was no way she wanted some hungry horse sticking its face in her hair! Claudia gently pushed Sadie's head away. "Let's head to the stable. I have some horses to introduce you to."

Katani slowly followed Claudia to the side of the stable where the two horses were tied up. Katani thought the brown, shiny leather saddles were beautiful.

"Katani, you're nice and tall," Claudia observed.

If she says anything about basketball I'm going to scream, Katani thought. Everyone she met assumed she played basketball, just like her sister Patrice. But the truth was, Katani wasn't very good at basketball, or even that interested in sports. She was always the kind of girl who stood in the back hoping that the ball wouldn't come to her.

But Claudia didn't say a word about basketball.

"Your long legs will go well with Penelope here," Claudia

said, patting the rump of a tall brown horse. "And I've got a special little guy for you, Kelley. His name is Wilbur. Would you like to come over and say hello?"

"Wilbur. Wilbur. Wilbur," Kelley chanted as she approached the little grey horse with the big soft eyes.

Claudia laughed. She knew that repeating Wilbur's name was a good sign. Tentatively, Kelley reached up and touched Wilbur's soft nose. He let out a soft whoosh. Kelley turned. "He's talking to me."

Mrs. Fields smiled. "Perhaps he is, sweetheart."

"We're going to start by grooming the horses," Claudia said, grabbing a box of brushes.

"Grooming?" Katani asked.

"Yes. First, we're going to curry their coats," Claudia slipped a brush over her hand.

"Curry? Isn't that a spice?" Katani asked.

"Yes, but this is a different kind of curry," Claudia explained, handing Katani an oval brush about the size of her hand. It had a wide band on the back and Katani slipped her hand inside.

"Are you left- or right-handed?" Claudia asked Kelley.

Kelley pulled away.

"She's left-handed," Katani said. She held up her hand to show Kelley how the curry fit over her hand.

"Before we ride the horses, we brush them all over," Claudia said.

"Why?" Katani asked.

"It's relaxing for us, but especially the horses. Also, it gets rid of any dirt or grit from the paddock. Besides, it doesn't feel good if the horse has grit or dirt between the saddle and their skin. It could rub 'em raw when we are riding."

Katani didn't want poor Penelope to have raw skin

because she hadn't done a good enough job of grooming.

"Don't worry, Katani. Penelope here knows you'll treat her just right. Why don't you start brushing her neck?"

As soon as Katani touched Penelope's neck, the horse shivered. It was freaky. Katani wanted to pull back her hand. She wanted to run from the stable and climb back into Big Blue and lock the door, but she was supposed to be setting a good example for Kelley. So, she put her hand back on the horse's neck and softly stroked it with the curry brush. The horse turned its head and its huge, bowling ball eye rolled sideways to see what her new friend was doing.

Katani took a step back.

"It's not going to bite me, right?" she asked softly, under her breath, hoping that Kelley couldn't hear her.

She did. "Bite. Bite. Bite away little horsie," Kelley repeated in a sing-song voice.

"No!" Claudia assured her. "Penelope here is a real lady." Claudia reached over and gave the horse another pat. "She's just getting used to you, just like you're getting used to her," Claudia said. Katani stepped forward and began patting Penelope's neck. "OK, girl, you're going to be my friend."

Claudia showed Kelley how to make long, strong strokes and told her to always brush the hair in the same direction. Claudia had Kelley come up and stand next to her. Together they brushed Wilbur, who stood perfectly still like the little gentleman that he was. When Kelley was finished, she threw her hands around the horse's neck and laid her head down on him. "Wilbur, Wilbur, Wilbur," she sighed.

Meanwhile, Katani paused as she reached Penelope's rump. "You want me to brush back here?"

Claudia chuckled at Katani's expression. "Don't worry. You'll have plenty of warning. But be careful to never stand directly behind a horse. They can't see back there and if they get scared, they might kick."

"Whoa." Katani made sure that she stayed to the side of Penelope as she brushed her rump with long, strong strokes.

As they brushed, Claudia told them that the girls would eventually learn to clean the hooves and saddle the horses. And of course, they would have to clean out the stalls, too.

Clean out the stalls? But there's HORSE GUCK in there and stuff, Katani grimaced. Brushing a horse was one thing, but shoveling horse poop was quite another.

But before she could think too much about this, Claudia called for two of her assistants to come and help the girls get started.

"We've got to get these horses saddled and get you girls mounted up."

"Mount ... Mountain grown—the richest kind," Kelley mimicked one of her favorite commercials.

Claudia chuckled as two women in jeans joined her. "Girls, I'd like to introduce you to our volunteers today— Samantha and Catherine."

"Hey! I'm Sam," the older of the two said raising her hand.

"Hi. Nice to meet you," Catherine said in a quiet voice. She held her hands behind her back. She seemed a little timid, Katani thought.

"Catherine is new," Claudia explained. "But Sam's been with us a long time, right?"

"Right!" Sam said with a big smile.

"You first, Katani," Claudia said, dragging a wooden box over to the side of the horse. "This is an English saddle, so you don't have a horn to grab onto, but with your long legs, I don't think it's going to be a problem. Step up on the box. Put your foot here in the stirrup and swing your other leg up and over."

Katani stood still as if she were rooted to that one spot.

"Sam and Catherine will make sure that Penelope holds still for you, not that she's one to be fidgety. Penelope is a good ole girl."

Penelope acted like she knew exactly what Claudia had said. She snorted and pawed the ground. Kelley jumped back and grabbed onto Katani. "I don't want to ride a real horse. I want to ride on the carousel. I want my pink-and-lavender horse. I don't like Penelope one bit! No, sir, not one bit!"

"Don't you worry about a thing, Kelley. Katani's going to show you just how easy this is. Before you know it, you will be riding like a real champ," Claudia said. "Come on Katani. Step right up here on the box."

Katani was trying to act brave for Kelley, but the truth was, she was scared to death. Brushing Penelope was one thing—but sitting on top of her was a whole 'nother thing. Suddenly, Penelope looked huge ... super huge. She looked over at her grandmother, hoping for a reprieve. But Mrs. Fields only mouthed the word "courage."

Katani tried not to think about how nervous she felt and instead concentrated on Claudia's directions. Katani put her left foot in the stirrup and swung her right leg over the horse, found the other stirrup, and settled into the saddle. She leaned forward, straightened her shoulders, and pressed her heels down in the stirrups.

"Hey, would you look at that?" Claudia said, letting loose with a long, low whistle.

"What?" Katani asked.

"You sure you've never been on a horse before?"

"No. Why?"

"You look good up there, Katani. Look at that Sam," Claudia said, motioning to Katani.

"Yup, I see," Samantha said, smiling up at Katani.

"See what?" Katani wanted to know.

"Come here, Catherine, I want to show you what's going on here," Claudia said, pulling Catherine closer to her.

Katani looked around, wondering what they were talking about.

"Now Katani here has what we call a 'good seat.' See how she's sitting with her spine straight? And notice her legs. They're bent at just the right angle. I think we might have a natural horsewoman here, girls. Katani, it usually takes me weeks—sometimes months—to teach students to sit the way you're sitting right now."

Katani was stunned. No teacher or coach had ever called her a natural at any sport. She reached down and patted Penelope's neck. She almost felt like crying. She saw Grandma Ruby's beaming face out of the corner of her eye. Kelley clapped her hands.

"Time to mount. Time to mount," Kelley said again.

"Yes, it's your turn, Kelley," Claudia said.

Kelley backed away.

"Come on, Kelley. It's OK. It's fun," urged Katani. Suddenly, she really did feel like a natural. Even Penelope's raising her hoof and twitching didn't bother her.

Kelley didn't have a box to stand on. She had a whole staircase with a railing on either side to help her up.

Katani also noticed that Kelley's horse didn't have an English saddle. It had a padded, bucket-shaped saddle that would keep her from falling out. With both assistants gently steadying and guiding Kelley, they eased her up onto Wilbur. Wilbur snuffled softly as if to say "Welcome aboard."

"Now Kelley, I'm going to lead your horse. Catherine and Sam are going to run alongside Wilbur so you don't have to be afraid. OK?"

Kelley's eyes widened and she nodded. She looked frozen with fear, but as the horse began to move, a hint of a smile was creeping onto her face.

But what about me? Katani thought. *Who's going to lead my horse? Who's going to run alongside me?*

"Now Katani, you need to make a giddyup sound," Claudia demonstrated, making a clicking noise with her tongue. "Then gently kick Penelope's sides with your heels."

"But won't that hurt? Will it make her mad?" she asked.

"Mad? Oh my goodness, no. Your legs and heels are one way you communicate with your horse; sounds and reins are the others. Now hold the reins loosely in your hands. Pull them this way to go right and this way to go left. Gently pull up on the reins to ask Penelope to slow down or stop."

"But … I'm not sure … I mean, I don't know …" Katani stammered. Suddenly, she didn't feel like a natural anymore.

"Go ahead," Claudia prodded. "Just make a cluck-cluck sound with your tongue and nudge her with your heels." The whole idea that an animal that was so big would listen to Katani and do what she wanted her to do sounded absurd. But Katani did what Claudia suggested.

She clucked her tongue and nudged Penelope's sides with her heels. As she did, she pulled the reins to the right. Immediately, Penelope lifted her head as if saying "I understand" and started moving toward the ring, happy to follow Wilbur and Kelley. Catherine and Sam walked alongside Kelley, encouraging her every step of the way.

Kelley shouted out to Katani, "I'm riding! I'm riding! Good Wilbur," she repeated proudly.

Katani had to smile. Maybe this would be really good for Kelley after all.

Once in the ring, Claudia called out to Katani to tell Penelope to stop.

Katani pulled gently back on the reins and Penelope slowed to a stop. It worked. The horse was actually doing what Katani wanted. Claudia jogged over to Katani with a big grin. "You are doing fabulously, Katani. I don't often get the autistic kids on the horse that first day," Claudia said. "But Kelley is lucky to have such a great peer role model."

Katani was pleased, even though she hated being referred to as Kelley's peer role model. It sounded so goofy. But, she listened intently as Claudia explained about how to use her thighs to grip the horse beneath her. Then she told Katani to go around the ring a few times and try out her skills.

The first time around felt awkward, but as she and Penelope started the second trip around the ring, Katani was filled with an exhilaration she had never felt before. This was fun! She reached down and patted Penelope on the neck. Claudia asked if she wanted to trot. Katani nodded yes. Claudia told her to press her heels into Penelope's side and say "trot." Penelope obeyed immediately. At first, Katani was bouncing up and down, but Claudia ran beside her and told her to lean forward and move up and down, using her legs to help. Within a minute, she was moving in rhythm with Penelope's gait. Katani focused her full concentration on what she was doing. This was the most excited she had been in her entire life. Katani heard herself laugh out loud when Kelley yelled, "You go, girlfriend!"

CHAPTER 9

❧

FIRST ... AND LAST TIME?

"MOM. MOM! I rode a horse. All by myself," Kelley said, bursting through the back door.

"I know you did, honey, and I want to hear all about it. But first, girls, go wash up. Dinner is on the table," Mrs. Summers said. She winked at Katani. They both knew that Kelley needed to settle down before telling her story or she would be dancing all over the house all night long.

It was almost seven by the time they arrived home, and Katani was starving. She smelled something delicious. Her heart gave a thump. Her mother had made her favorite dinner—pork tenderloin with apricot sauce, wild rice, and apple-and-walnut salad. Katani knew that was her mother's way of saying thank you for going with Kelley.

Katani was so hungry she just wanted to eat right away. She forgot all about the half-hour shower she had promised to take the moment she stepped in the door—washing her hands at the kitchen sink was good enough. Plus, it felt kind of sweet to still have Penelope and the smell of the barn on her clothes.

"My horse's name is Wilbur," Kelley said as she sat down. "Wilbur, Wilbur."

Then she recited the entire lesson, word by word, while the rest of the family ate.

Katani was impressed. Kelley managed to repeat every word Claudia had said, exactly the way she said it. Katani tried to add in her two cents, but Kelley corrected her. No one could get a word in edgewise. Finally, Mr. Summers took Kelley into the other room and settled her down with her favorite movie of the week, *Pocahontas*.

"It sounds like you girls had a wonderful time," Mrs. Summers said after father and daughter left the room.

"Yes," Grandma Ruby agreed. "It seems we have a budding equestrian in the family."

"Kelley?" Patrice cocked her head in surprise.

"Actually, I was talking about Katani," she said proudly.

"What exactly is an equestrian?" Patrice asked.

"An accomplished horseback rider," answered Grandma Ruby. "Ms. McClelland said that Katani is a natural. She wants Katani to take lessons with a group at the stables."

"She said that?" Katani asked.

Grandma Ruby nodded.

Katani looked over at Patrice, who to Katani's surprise, gave her a thumbs-up.

Katani remembered hearing Claudia say that she was a natural, but she thought maybe the instructor was just exaggerating to make her feel good. Hippotherapy is great, a jubilant Katani thought as she stood up and began clearing the table, but her mother said, "No, honey, you've done enough for today. Come give me a hug and go start on your homework. Patrice, you take over for your sister tonight." Mrs. Summers smiled proudly at her youngest daughter.

Katani straightened her shoulders and headed out of the kitchen. *Mmm, Penelope. You and I are going to rock,* she hummed to herself.

Patrice huffed, but one look from her mother and she was at the sink shoving the dishes into the dishwasher.

On her way out Katani overheard her grandmother say, "Nadine, you should have seen your daughter, she looked magnificent on that horse, and so in control. I was very proud of her."

Katani danced her way to her room, then suddenly remembered that she needed to ask her mom if she could buy some riding pants. Claudia told her she would be much more comfortable in them. Plus, she'd look really stylish. Even a used pair would be OK. Katani headed back, but she paused at the kitchen door because she could hear Grandma Ruby talking to her mother in hushed tones.

"Yes, Claudia McClelland told me that High Hopes' existence depends on state funding and that it may be cut. She is urging everyone who cares about the stable to write their representative and state senator. Here's a sample letter. But there is also a more urgent matter."

The worried tone in her grandmother's voice made Katani hesitate. She ducked back into the shadows near the living room.

From what Katani could hear, some government agency department was insisting that High Hopes upgrade their stable or else close down and move the horses to another facility. The nearest Claudia had found was two hours away.

"That's out of our driving range, I'm afraid," Mrs. Summers noted.

"I'm afraid you are right," Mrs. Fields sadly admitted.

"Her petition to the Variance Committee was denied.

Bottom line—if she doesn't come up with the ten thousand dollars to pay for the stable improvements, High Hopes will have no hope of staying open at its present location. She's sent an urgent plea to all the families to look for funding."

Katani couldn't believe her ears. Finally, something that she was interested in and would love to do … and it might be taken away from her.

She burst into the room. "That's not fair, Mom. The stable is really clean and the teachers take really good care of the horses. I want to take riding there and so does Kelley. She was so happy today. You should have seen her. She kept hugging Wilbur."

"Honey," Mrs. Fields interrupted. "It's the barn. The horses are well-cared for. Claudia makes sure of that, but the barn needs to be replaced. It's old and rickety."

"Great, I finally find some sport I could be good at and now there is no place for me to go to do it." She stormed out of the room.

ACCEPT NO SUBSTITUTES

Mr. Ramsey pulled up in front of the Beacon Street Movie House.

"Thanks, Maeve. You were a great help!" he said. They put fliers up in all the animal hospitals and shelters they could find.

"Yeah, thanks for coming with us, Maeve," Charlotte added, giving her friend's hand a squeeze before she got out of the car.

"See you tomorrow, Charlotte. And don't worry. We'll find the little guy … we'll visit every house and park in Brookline if we have to," Maeve pronounced. She waved good-bye to Charlotte and Mr. Ramsey as she got out of the car. She went in the side door of the theater and pounded up the stairs.

"Maeve? Is that you?" her mother called.

Maeve cringed. She could tell by her mother's tone that she wasn't happy.

"OK, young lady you have some explaining to do," Ms. Kaplan said.

On *I Love Lucy*, that usually meant something funny was about to happen. But Maeve had a feeling that there was nothing funny about this at all.

Maeve summoned up the most confused look she could possibly muster. What had her drama coach said about looking confused? Eyes wide, mouth slightly open. Bring hand up to your chest? Say "Moi?"

"What?" Maeve asked, trying to keep her voice steady.

"It's the second Monday of the month." Her mother crossed her arms.

"And ..." Maeve shook her head.

"Tutoring, young lady."

Maeve slapped her right hand over her mouth. "Oh my gosh. I can't believe I entirely forgot about tutoring today." She hated to think about how many times she forgot about her sessions with Matt. Maeve sat down at the kitchen table. "Mom, here's the deal. Charlotte looked so sad all day. She asked if anyone could help her look for Marty after school. I was the only one who could help her and her dad look. We went to all the shelters. I just completely forgot."

"Maeve, forgetting is one thing, but not calling and telling me where you are going is another. You know the rules. It's just too nerve-wracking for me if I don't know where you are. If you aren't where you're supposed to be, there's every reason that I might think you've been hurt—and that's my worst fear."

"I know, Mom. I'm so, so sorry, but I just couldn't imagine what it would be like for Charlotte coming home to the house and being all alone—no mother, no cat, and now, no Marty. The words, 'I'll go with you Charlotte' just popped out of my mouth."

It had seemed like the right thing to do then. However, now under her mother's disapproving glare, she knew she had made a huge mistake.

"You ARE telling me the truth, right? You weren't off with Dillon were you?" Ms. Kaplan demanded.

"No, Mom. You can call Mr. Ramsey yourself. Marty is lost and we have to find him. Charlotte has like lost her mind over this. She's barely speaking to Avery because she thinks it's Avery's fault. I just had to help."

"No word on Marty?" Her mother's voice softened. She knew how crazy all the BSG were over that little mutt.

"We put signs all over the neighborhood, and Mr. Ramsey even helped us put up a website. But nobody has called." Maeve leaned in to her mother and in a knowing tone said, "Personally, I'm very worried. Of course, I wouldn't tell Charlotte and Avery that, but it's not looking good."

Maeve's mom bit her lip. Her daughter's dramatic delivery sounded like a 40-year-old soap opera actress delivering bad news.

Maeve sensed her mother softening.

"Besides, Mom. I do know that every Monday I have tutoring. I just got distracted, is all. When one of the BSG is in trouble, I can't focus. I have to stay loyal. It's our motto."

"Maeve," her mother said in a stern schoolteacher voice. "I respect your loyalty to your friends, but going somewhere without calling me or your father is completely and totally unacceptable. And besides worrying about your safety, tutoring is expensive. I have to pay for it whether you show up or not. I am going to have to talk to your father about this."

Maeve nodded. She knew her mom was right. She wouldn't like it if her mom went somewhere and didn't tell her. "Mom, I promise you I will do everything I can to remember to call you." Suddenly Maeve's eyes widened. "Maybe I should wear a pink bracelet or something to help me remember to call the next time."

Maeve's mother looked at her daughter. She knew that her daughter's learning issues made it difficult for her to remember all the details of her schedule. She knew that she had to encourage any attempt of her daughter's to stay organized. "Maeve, I think the bracelet is a really good idea. Maybe we can go over to Razzberry Pink's store later on in the week and find something."

Maeve jumped up and gave her mother a big hug. She would try to do better. She really, really, totally would!

Suddenly, the phone rang.

"I'll get it," Maeve said, lunging for the phone. "Hello!"

"Hello, Maeve?"

"Charlotte?" She'd just dropped her off minutes ago. There must have been an important development.

"What is it?" Maeve asked.

"A shelter called and they found a dog matching Marty's description."

Maeve's heart began beating faster. "Is it one of the shelters we went to today?"

"No. It's on Freemont Street. I left a message on their answering machine on Sunday because it was too far to walk to. I don't have any way to get there, and I was wondering if your mom could possibly drive us. They're closing in about twenty minutes."

"Where's your dad?"

"He dropped me off at the house and went back to school to finish his last hour of office hours. I tried to call him, but he's not picking up his cell phone. He must be with a student."

"Hold on a second," Maeve said. This wasn't going to be easy. How was she going to convince her mom, who two seconds ago was grounding her, to drive her to this animal shelter? She covered the receiver of the phone. There was nothing to do but press on.

"Mom, it's Charlotte."

Her mother crossed her arms and raised one eyebrow.

Maeve took a deep breath and continued on. "Her father went back to work and she's there all alone. A shelter called. They think they found Marty. They close in twenty minutes. Mom, please. It's for Charlotte. Her father is with a student or something. She has no other family. Please, Mom. For Charlotte ... and for Marty."

"I'll drive you girls there. But don't be confused ... I'm doing this for Charlotte, not for you, young lady. Let me get my purse. Tell her we'll be right there."

RESCUE MISSION

Maeve could see Charlotte standing in front of her house waiting for them as they turned onto Corey Hill.

"Thanks, Mom. This means so much to Charlotte, you have no idea."

Charlotte waved to them as soon as she saw Ms. Kaplan's station wagon.

"Thank you so much, Ms. Kaplan—I really appreciate it. I printed the directions off the Internet so we wouldn't get lost." Charlotte handed the map and directions to Ms. Kaplan.

Ms. Kaplan looked at the directions. "Oh, I know just where this is," she said as she pulled away from the curb.

"I really appreciate this," Charlotte said again.

"It's quite all right, dear," Maeve's mother answered as she pulled away from the curb.

Charlotte buckled herself in. "Can you believe this! It's a good thing I got home when I did. I heard the phone ringing and ran upstairs. If your mom couldn't have taken us, we'd have to wait a whole day. Oh, I miss that little guy so much. I can't wait to get my hands on his chubby little self for worrying me like this."

"Did you bring his collar?"

"Yup," Charlotte said, pulling it out of her bag and his leash too, and a Baggie full of his favorite treats.

"I think we should plan a welcome home party for him tomorrow after school," Maeve said.

Ms. Kaplan cleared her throat. "Girls, I don't think you should get your hopes up. We don't know for sure that this dog is Marty." Maeve and Charlotte looked at each other and crossed their fingers. They hoped—no they believed—that in a few minutes Marty would be their arms.

"Maybe we could make the party later in the week ..." Maeve enthused. "We could have special dog treats for Marty and cool treats for us, too! And pictures. We definitely don't have enough pictures of Marty. It'll be a Celebrate Marty day, and we could go to the park and ..."

"And whatever we do," Charlotte interrupted, "we'll make sure this collar is on tight. Or maybe I'll buy him one of the halter things so he can't possibly wiggle out."

"He is a wiggler."

"We should have named him Houdini. He is the ultimate escape artist."

"Maybe that's how he got away from his first owner," Maeve said.

Charlotte looked stung.

"I mean, well, I guess not. He had his collar on when we found him."

Charlotte stared out the window.

"I've been thinking about that," Charlotte said. "For a while, I thought maybe Marty might have found his way home. His first home, I mean."

"Marty would never leave us …"

"But he did."

"I mean he would never leave us *on purpose*."

"Here we are girls," Ms. Kaplan said as she pulled to the curb in front of the Sawgrass Animal Shelter.

The girls tumbled out of the car and raced to the door with Ms. Kaplan following them up the steps.

Inside, Charlotte stepped up to the receptionist desk.

"I received a phone call from you," Charlotte started out a little timidly.

The girl at the counter stared at her, snapping her gum.

Charlotte continued. "You found a dog matching the description of my dog?"

"Oh, yeah. The little energetic mutt. Follow me."

The girls walked through the back door into a room with a concrete floor and rows of dogs behind chain link kennels. A large dog lunged at the fence, barking ferociously. Maeve jumped. She fell back against the chain link fence on the other side. The moment she touched it, another large dog jumped up behind her.

"Watch out for that one," the shelter worker warned, strangely unfazed.

Maeve pulled her arms in to the center of her chest and

carefully walked down the middle of the aisle away from either side of the fences. It seemed every dog in the kennel was barking now. It was a cacophony of soulful baying and shrill yipping. The girl from the front desk walked on as if she didn't hear a thing. Maeve wanted to cry. She never realized how many lost dogs there were. She tried to get Charlotte's attention, but Charlotte was anxiously scanning the cages.

In the back of the room, kennels were stacked for the smaller dogs.

Maeve listened for the little familiar snuffling bark that was distinctively Marty's, but she couldn't hear anything above the din.

"Here he is," the girl said, opening the middle cage and bringing out a small, shaking dog.

The little dog was gray like Marty. It had bent ears like Marty. It had big black eyes like Marty. But it was definitely NOT Marty.

Charlotte's heart sank.

"That's not him," she said dejectedly.

"Are you sure?" Ms. Kaplan asked. "He looks …"

Maeve gave her mother a weird look.

"I've only seen Marty a few times," Ms. Kaplan continued, "but I'd swear this is Marty. Perhaps he's just a little dirty. Maybe after you bathe him you'll see that it's him."

"Mom, believe it me. This dog is NOT Marty. If this dog were Marty, it wouldn't be cowering and shaking. He'd be dancing up a storm, wiggling right out of her hands, and covering both of us with kisses," Maeve explained.

"Maybe he's just a little shy, traumatized from being lost," Ms. Kaplan suggested.

"You want to hold him?" the girl asked and shoved the dog into Charlotte's arms before she could answer.

❁

The dog cuddled and nestled into the crook of Charlotte's arm, hiding his face from the rest of them. Just looking at the back of the dog, Maeve had to admit that the dog did look a lot like Marty.

"Oh, Charlotte! Are you sure? He seems to be comfortable with you," Ms. Kaplan said.

"Well, what's the verdict?" the girl asked.

"It's not Marty," Charlotte said sadly as she pet the shaking, quivering bundle of fur in her arms.

"Well, perhaps it's not Marty, but it's still a very nice little dog," Ms. Kaplan replied. She reached out and stroked the little puppy.

"He's the only quiet one of the bunch," the girl said as the other dogs in the kennel yapped and barked.

"How long has this dog been here?"

"He arrived this afternoon," the girl snapped through her gum.

"Well ... how long has Marty been gone?"

"Since Saturday afternoon," Charlotte replied, the words catching in her throat.

Maeve had seen that look on Charlotte's face before and thought perhaps she might burst into tears at any moment.

"It's not Marty," Maeve told her mother again.

No one moved, so Maeve took the Marty lookalike from Charlotte's arms and gave it back to the girl.

"Sorry, I really thought ..." the girl began, searching for the right words.

Charlotte hung her head and nodded. "It was really nice of you to call."

"Let's not be so hasty girls," Ms. Kaplan said, taking the dog from the girl and holding him up in the air. "Look at this little guy's face. What a cutie. He may not be Marty ... but he still needs a home."

"MOM!" Maeve exclaimed, taking the dog from her mother's arms and giving it back to the girl. "We came here for Marty. We don't need a substitute. We're going to find Marty. Come on, Charlotte," Maeve said, putting her arm around her dejected friend as they walked back through the room of barking and yapping.

They could still hear the dogs when they got in the car.

Charlotte was quiet the entire ride home. As soon as they dropped her off and pulled away from the curb, Maeve finally spoke.

"Mom, I can't believe how you were pushing that dog on Charlotte. She doesn't want *any* dog. She wants Marty," Maeve said.

"I know. I was only trying to help, and I felt so bad for that little dog. I hope someone adopts him," Ms. Kaplan said, glancing in the rearview mirror back at Maeve.

"Not just any dog can replace Marty."

Ms. Kaplan gave Maeve a reassuring smile. "I know that Marty is important to you girls, honey, but we have to be realistic here. The longer Marty is lost, the less likely it is that we will find him. And it would be dreadfully unfair to get Charlotte's hopes up and then have them dashed."

Maeve stared out the window. *Where had that little dude gone?* she wondered.

CHAPTER 10

ભ

GONE FOR GOOD?

WEDNESDAY MORNING was raw and gray. Charlotte stared out the window for a long time trying to motivate herself to get out of bed. Marty had only been gone less than five days, but Charlotte missed him so much it hurt. She never realized how much of her morning was spent with the little guy — walking him, feeding him, and playing with him. Now she felt alone.

As she packed up her backpack, she realized the school week was half over. Tuesday had come and gone with no word about Marty. She glanced at her watch ... he had been missing for ninety hours. Heading down Beacon Street, Charlotte hardly heard Yuri the grocer call to her.

"Hey, sad girl. You want apple, no?" Yuri called to her has she passed by the bins and tubs of fruit outside of his grocery store.

Charlotte really didn't feel like talking to anyone, but to pass by and not say anything would be rude.

"No thank you, Yuri," she said.

"Sad face tells me that the Marty dog is still missing,

no?" Yuri asked.

Charlotte couldn't say anything. She just nodded her head sadly. She told Yuri how she had built her hopes up so much on Monday night when the Sawgrass Animal Shelter had called. How she was sure that it was Marty. How she had rushed to the shelter and found not Marty, but another poor lost dog, who looked as sad as she felt.

This morning, Charlotte felt so bad that she called the shelter to check on the little dog. The receptionist had told her that the owner had shown up. She could just imagine the happy scene between the timid little dog and the owner. It made her happy to think that the dog was rescued, but it also made her jealous and depressed.

"Come, I have just the thing to cheer you up," Yuri said, motioning for Charlotte to follow him inside.

He picked up a reddish-orange colored fruit resembling a pear and polished it.

"Here," he said, placing it in her hand. "Guaranteed to put a smile on your face."

"What is it?" Charlotte asked.

"What matters the name …? You try."

Charlotte took a bite. The fruit was juicy and so good. Sweet. Juice trickled down her chin. Charlotte couldn't help giggling as she grabbed a napkin from Yuri's hand. The taste stayed in her mouth.

"See! Yuri's right, no?"

"What is it?" Charlotte asked as she took a second bite. She was ready for the juice this time.

"An Asian pear. Fruit of the gods."

Charlotte nodded and was glad she had left home fifteen minutes early so she had time to savor the Asian pear.

"See this," Yuri said. Yuri held up a bone. "This is best

soup bone in house. I've saved it for your four-legged friend. A celebration bone for his happy return."

"I don't know …" Charlotte shrugged. "I don't know Yuri. He's been gone so long. I'm not sure if he's ever coming back."

Yuri scoffed. "Dogs have built-in homing device. I've heard story of dog traveling halfway across the country. Incredible stories … in United States and also in Russia. Marty is smart one. That I know. "

"Thanks, Yuri. I hope you are right." She actually had a smile on her face as she continued on her way to school.

Dogstar

The day was as dismal as the weather. Charlotte passed from class to class without really hearing her teachers. Ms. Rodriguez stopped her in the hall and asked her if there had been any word about Marty. Charlotte shook her head and was relieved that all Ms. R did was pat her on the shoulder. She didn't want to keep her hopes up if Marty really wasn't going to be found. For the first time since she had come to Abigail Adams Junior High, Charlotte didn't eat lunch with the Beacon Street Girls. She went to the library instead. She was too sad to make chit-chat with Avery … or anyone else.

Later that afternoon when she got home, she rushed to check the answering machine. No messages. She checked the website. Nothing. She pulled her comforter and a big pillow out onto her balcony and watched the street below. In her reporter's notebook, Charlotte wrote down the sensations of eating an Asian pear—juicier than an apple, crisp, yummy. Perhaps she could use them in a poem later.

After dinner, Charlotte checked the website again. This time there was a message! Someone said they had found Marty! Her heart began to pound with excitement. She cautioned herself against getting her hopes up too high again. This might be another false alarm. But, she couldn't help herself. She was excited.

The message was from someone with the screen name Dogstar. Dogstar said that he had Marty penned in his yard because he was extremely allergic to dogs. Dogstar also wrote that he didn't have a car, so he couldn't bring Marty to them, but that Charlotte could pick up Marty anytime at the following address: 400 Weeble Street. *What a weird street name*, thought Charlotte.

Of course this would happen on a Wednesday when her father had not one, but two night classes. Charlotte text-messaged her father, hoping that he would check his cell phone between classes.

If only she could email her address to Dogstar. But she promised her father she would never email her address to anyone she didn't personally know. For now, all she could do was wait.

Charlotte nearly jumped when her cell phone rang. She stumbled over her book bag to reach it and stubbed her toe. All her father could hear was Charlotte groaning. "Charlotte, honey, what's the matter? Talk to me."

She was half in pain and so excited she could barely get the words out.

"Dad! Dad! I stubbed my toe but someone called Dogstar found Marty! They left a message on the website. Can you come home between classes so we can go get him?"

"Charlotte, I can't. My next class starts in twenty minutes."

"Well, then after class?"

"Charlotte, it's not going to work. I won't be home until 10:30 and that is too late. How about you email the person and tell them that we'll pick up Marty when I get home from work tomorrow? I'll even come home early and pick you up at school."

"Tomorrow? Dad, Marty will be outside. We can't wait that long."

"Listen Charlotte, I don't have time to quibble. Class is about to start. See ya tonight. Bye."

Before Charlotte could say good-bye, he had hung up. She didn't even have time to tell him she didn't have a phone number for Dogstar. Only a street address and email address.

"Oh, darn," grumbled Charlotte. Well, at least Marty would be home soon. It just couldn't be another false alarm. Charlotte went back online and was happy to see that the BSG were online too.

Chat Room: BSG

File Edit People View Help

skywriter: great news!!!!
lafrida: what??????
4kicks: tell me someone found marty
flikchic: that true? is marty with you now?
4kicks: can i come c him?
skywriter: hold on! not that simple
lafrida: what??????
4kicks: i CAN'T come c him?
skywriter: marty's not here
4kicks: but i thought you said ...

4 people here

skywriter
lafrida
4kicks
flikchic

skywriter: I'll start over
... POSSIBLE great news

lafrida: what??????

skywriter: email from
dogstar. dogstar has marty

4kicks: where

skywriter: in his backyard

4kicks: well go get him!!

skywriter: can't no car. dad
at work

flikchic: mayB i can help

skywriter: nope. dad says
after school

4kicks: after school?!

skywriter: i know. wish we
could go sooner

lafrida: how 'bout b4 school?

skywriter: dad has early
class. doesn't want me to go
alone

4kicks: no sweat. i'll go
with u

skywriter: really? great!

4kicks: wanna meet at
montoya's

skywriter: ok at 8

flikchic: i'll start
planning the welcome home
party

4 people here

skywriter
lafrida
4kicks
flikchic

CHAPTER 11

❧

THE TREASURE HUNT

"YOU'RE UP EARLY?" Mrs. Madden said as Avery came rushing down the stairs.

"I'm meeting Charlotte for breakfast at Montoya's. To ... to ... talk about a new strategy for finding Marty," she stammered. "I gotta run. I'm late." She gave her bemused mom a quick hug and was out the door.

Avery slammed the door and took off at full speed. She didn't slow down until she turned onto Beacon Street. She couldn't be late this morning, not when Charlotte was waiting to go and get Marty. The early morning streets were busy with cars and people on their way to work, and Montoya's was bustling with a line for coffee that went out the door.

Avery hadn't eaten anything yet and her stomach growled when she smelled the fresh muffins and donuts.

Charlotte was already there waiting at a table.

"Did you order already?" Avery asked.

"No. They're really busy. So, we won't have time. We need to get to Dogstar's early so we aren't late for school," Charlotte said with firm determination.

Avery couldn't tell if Charlotte was eager to go after Marty or was still mad at her. Either way, Avery was going to be on her best behavior. She missed Marty and needed Charlotte's support. Charlotte was still speaking to Avery, but Char's warm friendliness seemed to have disappeared.

"You did eat before you came, didn't you?" Charlotte asked pointedly.

Avery's stomach growled again. "No, I thought we were eating here first. You know, then we'd make a game plan to go and rescue Marty. I mean, Charlotte, we don't really know these people."

Charlotte stared at her friend. "You don't have to come, you know."

"I'm coming," Avery said firmly. She was beginning to get annoyed, too. After all, it was Charlotte who hadn't put Marty's collar on tight enough.

"It's almost a mile there, then a mile back to put him safely in my house and then off to school. We don't have time to eat."

"OK." Avery shoved her hands in her pockets and leaned back in the chair.

"What can I get for you?" Nick asked, swinging a chair backwards and taking a seat.

"Hi, Nick. You're working before school now?" Avery asked, relieved for the interruption. Besides, she really, really wanted a muffin!

"Not really. I just came to help Mom unload the delivery truck. I finished about fifteen minutes ago, but it was so busy, she asked me to help out," Nick explained. "What are you guys doing here so early?"

"Last night, we got a message on the website about Marty. Someone has him in their backyard. They live in the 400 block of Weeble Street."

"Weeble Street—I have never head of it. You guys aren't going there by yourselves, are you?" Nick asked.

"Yeah," Avery admitted. "But it's only a mile."

"We really have to get going," Charlotte said.

"Please, Charlotte. I'm starved. Can't we get something to eat?" Avery pleaded.

"Hold on, Avery." Nick jumped up and ran behind the bakery counter. He grabbed some sugar-coated donuts and stuffed them in a bag. He was back to the table in a flash.

Avery flashed him a grateful smile and stuffed a dollar in his hands.

Charlotte smiled at Nick. He always seemed to do the right thing without being a goody-goody.

"So what's the name of the people on Weeble Street?" Nick asked Charlotte.

"I don't actually know. Their screen name was Dogstar."

"They have a screen name of Dogstar, but they said in the message that they're allergic to dogs? How weird is that?" Avery asked.

Charlotte shrugged. "I guess. I didn't think of that."

"You got this address online? And you don't know who these people are?" Nick asked. "Do your parents know you're going?"

Avery and Charlotte looked at each other and shook their heads no.

Nobody said anything for a minute.

Nick stood up. "This sounds suspicious. I'm coming along. In case you need someone to, you know, protect. Help." Nick disappeared around the line of people at the counter and into the back room.

"Protect us?" Avery asked. "From what?"

Charlotte blushed. "I don't know. But he is really nice."

"Whatever," Avery said. She opened her bag and began snarfing down her donut. If they were going dog hunting, she needed energy.

Nick was back in a second and the group took off out the front door and up Beacon Street.

"Didn't want anyone to see me bring this out," Nick said, pulling a white bag from inside of his coat and handing it to Avery. "They're hot from the oven. But it's better than listening to your stomach growl all morning, Ave."

Avery peeked in the bag.

"Biscotti! Now that's what I'm talking about," Avery exclaimed. "You're the man, Nick!"

☙

Halfway to Boston University, Mr. Ramsey realized that he left behind the papers he had just finished grading for his freshman writing class. *I better go back and get those future gems of literature* he smiled to himself. *I promised my students I would hand them back today.* The vision of impatient students frothing at the mouth for their grades impelled him to make a quick left turn on to Harvard Street and rush home.

He left his car in front of the yellow Victorian and raced up the stairs. His papers were sitting in the hall. He placed them carefully into his briefcase, and then he suddenly had a thought. *It will be such a nice surprise to have Marty waiting at home when Charlotte gets back from school.* He checked his watch … still an hour and a half until his first class. Mr. Ramsey turned on his computer and checked the address posted by Dogstar on www.wheresmarty.com. *Might as well give it a try*, he thought.

☙

On the way to Weeble Street, Charlotte relayed Marty stories to Nick and confessed that she just couldn't face losing another pet. Avery wasn't paying much attention to the conversation. She really didn't know where they were going and hoped Nick and Charlotte did. This was a part of Brookline that she didn't come to very often. She was content to follow along behind them scarfing one biscotti after another.

"Hey, Sugar Face," Charlotte called out. "You might want to brush yourself so you can make a good impression."

Avery wadded up the bag and stuck it in her backpack. She wiped her face off with a napkin and then brushed the crumbs from her coat. When she looked up she felt a little uneasy at her new surroundings.

The street was lined with old brick apartment buildings, but it was vacant and a tad creepy. Charlotte wondered if anyone actually lived on the street at all.

"I wonder how Marty wound up here?" Avery asked.

"Does that building have a number on it?" an obviously nervous Charlotte asked.

"Yeah," Avery said. "It's number 380."

"They've been skipping by twenties so the next building should be four hundred," Nick said.

They walked by a vacant lot and came up on the building on the other side. The numbers 420 prominently displayed over the doorway.

"Four twenty? But that can't be. That means that the vacant lot is 400 Weeble Street," Avery said.

"I think we should get out of here," Nick said looking around anxiously.

"Wait! Look! There on top of that old dumpster," Avery shouted and sprinted in that direction.

"Ave, wait!" Nick shouted. "This could be dangerous."

Too late, Avery was running toward the dumpster. What was the thing on top? It almost looked like it was a dog. A dog? *It couldn't be Marty,* she thought. There was no way that Marty would sit still for that long. Avery looked up.

"Avery!" She heard Charlotte call. "What is it?"

On the dumpster sat an old tattered stuffed animal that looked a little like Marty. Pinned to the front was a copy of their flier and written in tiny letters on the front of the flier was a message from Dogstar.

"What does it say?" Charlotte asked again. "Does it say where Marty is?"

Avery squinted to read it. Perhaps Charlotte was right. Maybe there was a clue about where Marty really was. Was this some kind of crazy treasure hunt? Avery wondered.

Grabbing the note, Avery began to read it out loud: "Disappointed? So is your little dog. Your dog ran away because it was too embarrassed to be seen with someone as weird as you."

"It says that? Really?" Charlotte said, pulling the note from Avery's hand so she could read it herself. She sucked in her breath. Somebody thought she was weird. Charlotte felt sick to her stomach. She handed the dog and the note over to Nick.

"What kind of creep would write something like that?" Avery asked. Furious, she wanted to wad the note into a tight little ball and throw it right through the side of the dumpster.

"This dude is so mean!" Nick slapped his hand against the dumpster.

"Three guesses who did this," Avery growled.

"You're kidding. You think A & J ... *did this*?" Nick asked. "No way. They're not this bad."

"Avery might be right, Nick," Charlotte said. "Anna and Joline love making other people miserable, and they did take fliers on Monday."

"I'm throwing this away," Avery said, opening the top of the dumpster. "I don't care who did it. It's nasty and I don't want any part of this."

"No wait. I think we should keep it as evidence. Maybe we can figure out from the handwriting who wrote it," Charlotte said.

"What's the point?" Avery mumbled. "Like you're going to call the FBI and then arrest them. Besides, it will just waste our time. We don't want to forget about Marty."

"I still think we should keep it," said Charlotte. Maybe it was the reporter or detective in her, but Charlotte really wanted to know who did this and why.

"You know what? What goes around comes around," Nick said wisely. "Whoever did this is just a low person. And that will come back to haunt them somehow. We better head off to school. It's getting late."

Just as they were turning to leave, a familiar car pulled into the lot, and a very worried-looking Mr. Ramsey jumped out of the driver's seat.

"Uh-oh," Charlotte said quietly, "This is not good. Not good at all."

"We're busted," Avery whispered.

"Charlotte ... you have some explaining to do," said Mr. Ramsey sternly.

"Mr. Ramsey, we just wanted—" Avery started to say.

"Dad, we *really, really* wanted to get Marty home. We miss him so much. I'm so sorry ... I know you told me to wait. It turns out this was all a mean trick. Look," Charlotte said, and showed her dad the note.

Mr. Ramsey didn't even look at the note. "You are all smart kids, but this was a really stupid thing to do, coming here all alone. I'm disappointed in all of you. I know you want to get Marty back, but you should not have put yourselves in danger to do that. Avery and Nick, I am going to have to call your parents."

Charlotte looked down at her feet. She knew she had messed up big time, plus she got her friends in trouble too.

As they rode back in disappointed silence, Avery couldn't stop thinking about Marty. She hoped wherever he was, that someone was being good to him. And although Avery was furious that they had been tricked, she wondered how Anna and Joline could really be this mean.

CHAPTER 12

CR

WINNING STREAK

"HI GUYS!" Maeve sang out. "Whatcha looking at?"

She stopped by the boys' lunch table—conveniently located right next to the BSG lunch table. The guys were leaning over the sports section from this morning's edition of *The Boston Globe*.

"Did you see this? Hey, check out Robbie Flores."

"Oooh, he's so cute," Maeve said, fixing her eyes on the picture of Flores swinging the bat.

"Cute? This player is strong! It says here he can bench press 200 pounds," Pete said.

"Wow," Maeve said. "Is that a lot?"

"Wanna come to the gym after school and find out?" Pete challenged Maeve.

"I don't think so," Maeve raised her chin. Boys were so competitive about their muscle power. It could be so annoying.

"Flores really found his rhythm again," Pete added.

Avery walked up and slapped her super sub sandwich down on the table. "Who found his rhythm again?"

"Flores," Dillon responded.

"Isn't it great!" Avery said, unwrapping her sandwich. "He was doing awesome this summer. Third in the League in hitting and fifth in RBIs and then—POOF!—he went into a slump. But he's found his groove again."

"What's the reason for the big turnaround?" Maeve asked.

"He says he has a lucky charm."

"Lucky Charms? Like the cereal?" Maeve couldn't believe a batting slump had anything to do with a box of cereal.

"I doubt he's talking about marshmallows," Pete chuckled.

"You mean a grown man believes in lucky charms?" Maeve asked.

"Are you kidding me? Athletes are some of the most superstitious people on the planet," Dillon told her.

"Especially baseball players," Pete added.

"Like David Ortiz," Dillon said.

"And Pedro Martinez," Avery mumbled through a bite of her sub sandwich.

"And don't forget Manny Ramirez," Dillon reminded the group.

"What kind of lucky charms do they believe in? Like carrying a rabbit's foot or four-leaf clover or something?" Maeve wondered.

"All kinds of things," Dillon answered.

"So what's Robbie Flores' lucky charm?" Maeve asked.

"It's a mystery. That was one of the points of the article, he's claiming his newest streak is due to a lucky charm, but he won't say what it is," Joey said, pointing to the article.

"Well, whatever his lucky charm is, it sure is working," said Avery. "Flores is on fire and the Sox are two games up on the Yankees."

"Yeah, but the Yankees come to town this weekend for a four-game series," Billy reminded them.

"Don't worry, don't worry," Dillon said. "The Yankees are going down!"

"Yeah right, the Red Sox will blow it this year again for sure," said Danny Pellegrino, the lone Yankee fan in Ms. Rodriguez' class.

"Whatever, Pellegrino," Peter responded, "Schilling's starting on Thursday and there's no way he's losing."

"Come on Avery, I'm starved," Maeve said as the boys launched into the Red Sox vs. Yankees debate they had every day. Maeve thought all this baseball talk was getting to be really boring.

"Be there in a minute," Avery answered, chomping at her sandwich. She wanted to talk more about Robbie Flores. A nice bit of sports wrap-up would help her forget about this morning's fiasco.

Maeve walked away. *Avery may want to hang out with the guys, but I'm going to sit down and eat like a civilized movie star,* she thought.

PICTURE PERFECT

Avery glanced over at the BSG table. Maeve motioned for her to come, but Avery mouthed, *in a minute.* She really didn't want to leave just yet, but she didn't want to offend the BSG either. After all, she was on shaky ground these days with Charlotte. Even though she'd gone along with Charlotte to the vacant lot this morning, Char was still acting distant. Avery missed the sensitive, kind Charlotte she used to know. It was as if the loss of Marty had turned her into another person.

"Come on, Pellegrino, Flores is way better than Jeter," Peter argued.

"Well, you might like a streaky hitter, but Jeter has batted over 300 all year, and he's the best clutch hitter in baseball,"

Danny replied.

"What!" exclaimed Avery. "No way … Big Papi is hands down better in the clutch."

Avery liked talking sports with her guy friends. There just weren't that many girls who knew all the Red Sox stats, or cared, for that matter. And right now it took her mind off other things.

Avery listened intently as Dillon read a brief article about the Sox pitching staff. When he laid down the paper, Avery leaned in close to get a better look at the box score, but got distracted by something she saw in a photograph of the Sox dugout. She blinked. What was that in the dugout? She grabbed the paper and ran off.

"Where's Ave going in such a hurry?" Isabel asked Maeve.

"Probably went to call the reporter to complain about the sports coverage," laughed Maeve.

"I wasn't finished reading that!" Dillon shouted after her.

"I'll bring it back," Avery called over her shoulder.

Suddenly the bell rang ending lunch period and the girls raced to gather their things before the next bell rang. Somehow, Charlotte ran into Avery who was racing back into the lunchroom carrying a magnifying glass. "Oh, Charlotte, you have to see this," she said excitedly. Suddenly, Avery was pushed into Charlotte who bumped into Anna and Joline, who tried to shove past them.

"Hey, watch it!" Avery shouted.

"Watch it yourself, shrimp," Anna shot back.

"Hey, we know what you did," Avery retorted.

Anna turned around. "What do you mean?"

"What do I mean?! Charlotte, Nick, and I didn't think your little trick this morning was funny at all."

"Trick? What trick?"

"The stuffed dog. The nasty note. Hellllllllooooooo!" Avery said, pretending to knock on the side of Anna's head. "Anyone home?"

"I don't know what you're talking about," Anna winced, batting Avery's hand away.

"Oh, please—so Dogstar means nothing to you," Avery put her hands on her hips.

Joline and Anna looked at Avery like she was demented.

"Oh, 400 Weeble Street means nothing to you," Charlotte said, stepping up to defend her friend. She might be annoyed with Avery, but having Anna and Joline dis Avery was a whole other thing.

"Where's that?" Joline asked.

"Don't play dumb with us. You know perfectly well that's where you left that stuffed dog on the dumpster ..." Avery said.

"We don't know what you're talking about." Joline looked genuinely confused.

Charlotte started to get nervous. Joline seemed sincere. What if they weren't the ones that played such a low trick after all ...?

The crowd shuffling around the four girls slowed as everyone turned to listen to the drama unfold outside the lunchroom door.

"So, what exactly are you talking about?" Anna asked, standing face to face with Avery.

"The dumpster, the message on the website, the stuffed dog, the note pinned on the stuffed dog," Avery said. "You two are the only ones we know mean enough to think up a trick like this."

"The note was the giveaway," Charlotte said, pulling it out of her bag. "Looks like your handwriting," she added, shoving the note in front of Anna.

Anna gasped as if she had been hit across the face. "I didn't write that note!" She turned to her friend. "Joline?"

Joline looked like she might cry. "I love dogs," she sniffed.

Anna looked mad. "If you want to go to the circus go buy a ticket," she hissed at the gathering crowd.

Charlotte was confused. Had she and Avery made a terrible mistake? Ever since Marty disappeared things had spun out of control. She was mad at Avery, she went somewhere without telling her dad, and now she was in the hall fighting with the Queens of Mean.

Mrs. Treadway, the lunchroom attendant, pushed her way through the crowd to the four girls. "OK! On your way, everyone! All of you!"

The crowd, which had been silent before, began to buzz with excitement as the students started to move again.

"What are they talking about?"

"What did Anna and Joline do?"

Everyone wanted to know what was going on.

Katani said it wasn't anybody's business and to "forget about it."

While the hall was clearing out, Anna made her way back across to Avery.

"You are so wrong, Avery. You think we would waste our time thinking about you or your stupid dog? Never." Anna flipped her hair and walked away. Joline looked sad and defeated.

Avery didn't even notice Joline's face. "Charlotte, you have to see this. You won't believe ..."

Charlotte cut her off. "I have to get to class Avery. Now."

Later that afternoon, on her way into art, Charlotte was handed a note that she should come straight to Ms. R's office. As she walked down the empty hall, she was feeling optimistic. Maybe Ms. Rodriguez had a new assignment for her for *The Sentinel*. However, the minute Charlotte saw Avery sitting in the teacher's office with a funny look on her face, she knew that it had nothing to do with the newspaper. Avery was sitting on her hands. She squirmed impatiently as she waited for Charlotte to sit down beside her.

"Charlotte, please take a seat," Ms. Rodriguez gestured to the chair.

Ms. Rodriguez sounded very serious and somber. Ms. R was Charlotte's favorite teacher and she hoped she hadn't let her down. Charlotte bit her lip and sank into the wooden chair next to Avery.

"I heard you two had a little altercation outside the lunchroom with Anna and Joline today," Ms. Rodriguez said.

"Altercation?" Avery asked.

"A fight," clarified Charlotte.

"It was more like a shouting match," Avery said.

Charlotte nodded.

"Well … Anna came to me about it. She was quite upset. It seems you made some accusations about them luring you to some dumpster this morning?"

Charlotte looked at Avery, who had sat up and was looking like her usual feisty self again.

"Yeah … it was a totally weird neighborhood," Avery explained to Ms. R.

"With a fake address," Charlotte added.

"Ask Nick! He went with us," Avery suggested.

"We got a message on the website that my dad set up …

someone named Dogstar said he had Marty. We shouldn't have gone there alone, but we wanted to get Marty back right away," Charlotte said. "When we got to the address, we found a stuffed dog with this note attached," she explained, pulling the note from her bag. "My dad was really upset. He came out there because he saw the message too."

Ms. Rodriguez looked at the note.

"It looks like Anna's handwriting," Charlotte said shakily. A hint of doubt was beginning to surface in her mind.

"And Anna and Joline both took a stack of fliers with them on Monday," Avery reported.

Ms. Rodriguez took a deep breath. "And what if it isn't Anna's handwriting?"

Charlotte felt her face flush. She looked up at Ms. R and said in a soft voice, "Then we made a horrible mistake accusing them in front of everyone."

"But we have proof," Avery said. "Look at the note!"

"I'm afraid this *doesn't* prove anything," Ms. Rodriguez said, handing the note back to Charlotte. "Lots of kids took fliers and this could be anyone's handwriting."

The room was quiet. Charlotte could hear the florescent light buzzing above them.

"I know that losing your dog has made the last week very tough for all of your friends, but you owe Anna and Joline an apology," Ms. Rodriguez said.

"What?" Avery gasped.

"Accusations without solid proof are extremely dangerous. You can easily damage a person's reputation. And it was especially unfair to make a scene in front of your classmates in the cafeteria. I expect to see a copy of your apology note on my desk by tomorrow. Do you girls understand?" Ms. Rodriguez said firmly.

✿

"Yes," Avery and Charlotte mumbled at the same time.

"Now, I have something for both of you. It's a note to your parents. They need to know all about this incident and why it happened. I know Charlotte's father is already aware of what happened this morning, but making false accusations will not be tolerated."

"Awww!" Avery put her hand to her forehead. "My mother is going to be so mad at me."

Charlotte just shook her head. Her dad wouldn't be as mad as he would be disappointed. She wished she could just turn back the clock to the day of the festival. Then she'd just leave Marty home and none of this would have happened.

"Avery, you may return to class. Charlotte, please stay," Ms. Rodriguez said.

Avery gave Charlotte a dejected look and left the room.

Ms. Rodriguez waited until the door was pulled closed tightly before she said anything. "Charlotte, what happened here? You are a journalist in training. Haven't we talked about the importance of objectivity and fact-gathering?"

Charlotte didn't know what to say, but she felt an urge to make some kind of explanation to her favorite teacher. "Ms. R, ever since Marty disappeared I just haven't been myself. I've been so angry at Avery for not paying close enough attention and I acted very irresponsibly this morning. I just wish Marty would come back." Then, without warning, Charlotte burst into tears. After a minute or two, Ms. R handed her a tissue. Charlotte sniffed a few more times and finally looked up at a teacher whose large brown eyes were filled with sympathy.

"This has been the most awful week of my life since I came to Boston," she whimpered.

"Charlotte, I am so sorry about your little dog. But, you need to stay more focused. Going to that address without an adult was a very dangerous thing to do."

Charlotte nodded. She could feel her cheeks turning bright red again.

"How is your piece for the paper coming?" Ms. Rodriguez changed the subject.

Charlotte was grateful to talk about something else.

"OK."

"Any problems?"

"None I can't handle."

Ms. R gave Charlotte a warm smile. "I suggest that you return to class then."

"Thank you, Ms. Rodriguez." Charlotte turned before she exited the room and added, "I'm sorry." Ms. Rodriguez' words haunted Charlotte. She was a feature writer for *The Sentinel*. She hoped that accusing Anna and Joline wouldn't jeopardize her position on the paper. That would be too terrible for words.

By the end of the day, Charlotte had to agree with Ms. R— anyone could have left the message on the website and left the dog and note on the dumpster. The fliers were all over town. They had left stacks at all their favorite shops. Anyone in Brookline could have picked one up. But when the final bell rang and Charlotte made her way to her locker, she still couldn't think of anyone mean enough to do such a thing. She knew it was unfair, but she couldn't quite get the notion out of her mind that Anna and Joline had something to do with the "dumpster incident." After all, being mean was their specialty.

"Charlotte, are you OK?" Maeve asked as she rushed up to Charlotte, who was closing her locker. "Avery told me all about what happened in Ms. Rodriguez' office. I can't believe that Ms. R would take Anna and Joline's side against you and Avery!"

"Well, she was sort of right. We shouldn't have accused them like that without more proof. And, we really shouldn't have done it in front of everyone. It really was kind of unfair of us, Maeve."

Maeve couldn't believe Charlotte was being so reasonable. She didn't trust the Queens of Mean at all and was sure they had something to do with putting the stuffed dog on the dumpster. It was just their style. But, she didn't say anything. If Charlotte wanted to be reasonable, that was up to her.

Katani came rushing over. "I just heard," she said. "Do you think your dad is going to be really mad?"

"Oh, yes." Charlotte shook her head up and down vigorously. "But even worse, he's going to be really disappointed. Especially after what we pulled this morning."

Katani nodded sympathetically. There would be big trouble in the Summers house if she ever pulled anything like Nick, Charlotte, and Avery did … lost dog or no lost dog!

"Do you need help after school?" Isabel asked as she approached Charlotte's locker. "Anything I can do to help find Marty?"

"I'm not sure what to do next," Charlotte said.

"I say we meet in the Tower and map out a plan," Maeve said. "Where's Avery?"

"What's going on?" Avery asked as she joined the group.

"We decided to go to the Tower to map out a Marty rescue plan," Maeve said.

"I can't make it," an apologetic Katani said. "I'm going back to the stables with Kelley this afternoon. Keep me posted though." Katani waved good-bye and took off toward Mrs. Fields' office.

Charlotte remained silent as Avery, Maeve, and Isabel

discussed every detail of the "A & J episode" during the walk home.

"OK! That's it," Charlotte exclaimed as she climbed the steps to her front porch. "I don't want to hear the names *Anna and Joline* anymore. I want to leave this whole issue at the doorstep. From here on out, let's just focus on finding Marty."

Charlotte opened the door and the girls tromped up the stairs to the second-floor living room.

Avery yelped with excitement.

The message light was blinking. Charlotte rushed over and hit the play button.

"You have one new message," the answering machine announced. "Friday. Two-fifteen …"

The answering machine message started playing. It was fuzzy at first, as if the person on the other end of the phone was outside. Charlotte could hear voices in the background. Then a man's voice started talking. He had a foreign accent. "Hello. I want you to know your dog, your little dog, is safe. He no hurt." There was a long pause and all the girls rushed to the machine.

"What?" Avery asked. "What did he say?"

"SHHHHH!" the other girls shushed in unison, staring at the answering machine, hoping there was more.

"I no want reward. In fact I pay you a hundred times that amount to keep dog. Call me at 555-0147," the man said hurriedly and then hung up.

❀

```
To: Charlotte
From: Sophie
Subject: Marty

ma cherie-

this is terrible news. my heart bleeds
for you. do not worry, ma cherie. this
will be different. you will see. cats are
independent ones--footloose and fancy
free. but dogs are very, very social.
they need people. i'm certain marty will
find his way home. let me know the minute
he arrives at your doorstep.
Ton amie, Sophie
```

Charlotte's Journal

Boy, did Avery, Nick, and I mess up! When my dad showed up at the vacant lot and found out that we went to look for Marty without an adult, he was furious. On top of that, I had to give him the note from Ms. R about the A & J incident. He actually yelled at me, even longer than when I was 9 and racked up a $127 phone bill talking to my friend Anabel in Australia.

Dad told me that we should all be old enough to know better. I HATE letting him down. He said that he had no idea what a proper punishment for this sort of thing was. He said he was going to ask the head of the ed department at the university. I hope he's kidding. I really don't want to have to scrub floors, or write a thousand word article on the dangers of being stupid!

Although I know now that it was a really, stupendously

dangerous thing to do, going to a strange place alone—because you never know what crazy people might be around. WE might have been kidnapped. I wasn't thinking straight (neither were Nick and Avery)—I was so worried about Marty that I forgot my common sense.

It was horrible today seeing that stuffed animal on top of the dumpster. And I did really think it was our adorable little Marty at first. My heart felt like it had stopped for a moment. Well, just for a second.

The whole thing was weird. I mean arriving at the address and not finding a building. Not finding Marty in the backyard like Dogstar said we would.

And then finding that dirty, tattered stuffed animal and that awful, hateful note. I just can't think of anyone else besides the Queens of Mean that would be that mean except for Kiki Underwood. But she is such a princess she would never touch something dirty or tattered. She would probably faint or throw a diva tantrum if she did.

The only good part of the whole morning was that Nick came with us. It was so sweet of him to think we needed help. And Avery was brave, too. I hope Avery and Nick didn't get into too much trouble. This whole thing is turning into one big mess.

File Edit People View Help

skywriter: hi guys

4kicks: hey char ... did you get in big trouble?

skywriter: My dad made a lot of noise and said he needed to think about what he was going to do ... U?

4kicks: mom was SO MAD i lied 2 her & coz it was dangerous. And she said it was completely unfair to blame A & J. She was gonna take me to get new bball shoes 2day but she's making me wait 2 weeks and she says I have to help Carla clean the house for the next two Saturdays

montoya33: my dad gave me an extra shift at the bakery this weekend—he said we shoulda known better. But he also was happy that I didn't let you two helpless girls go alone

4kicks: ug, I might be sick

skywriter: lol Nick. my dad said that 2 about knowing better

6 people here

skywriter
4kicks
montoya33
lafrida
Kgirl
flikchic

File Edit People View Help

4kicks: yup mom kept saying it was soooo stupid

lafrida: sounds like you 3 had a tough day

Kgirl: seriously

skywriter: yeah, not the best day ever. I'm really sorry Ave & Nick ... I begged my dad not 2 call

montoya33: it's not ur fault ... parents are like that. coulda been worse, something coulda happened 2 us

skywriter: dad was really angry that a person would play such a dangerous trick. He sent a legal email to Dogstar 2nite

montoya33: r u serious?

flikchic: go mr. ramsey!

skywriter: yeah---he said he wanted to get to the bottom of it. so he asked a lawyer friend to write the email. a half hour later he got a response ... from some kid

Kgirl: so it WASN'T anna and joline?

skywriter: nope ... my dad

6 people here

skywriter
4kicks
montoya33
lafrida
Kgirl
flikchic

scared the kid with his email ... the kid said he was so, so sorry and that it was just a practical joke

montoya33: is your dad gonna call the police?

skywriter: no ... he sent an email back to the kid saying that he wouldn't report him this time, but that the kid should never do something like that again

4kicks: guess it WAS a moronic idea to go alone, and we were fooled ... no Marty :-(

skywriter: yeah. the longer Marty's gone, the less likely we'll ever find him

4kicks: don't say that, we HAVE 2 find him

montoya33: that little dude will find his way back ... don't give up yet. see you girls tomorrow

4kicks: later nick

skywriter: hey bsg ... I have a new amendment to propose

6 people here

skywriter
4kicks
montoya33
lafrida
Kgirl
flikchic

6 people here

skywriter
4kicks
montoya33
lafrida
Kgirl
flikchic

Kgirl: go for it

flikchic: we're all ears

skywriter: We will never
listen to a stranger who
tells us to go someplace
without an adult ... it's
always a bad idea

lafrida: yeah today is an
example

4kicks: one of the best
amendments yet

Kgirl: I agree

flikchic: good thinking,
Char

4kicks: I have to show you
something important

skywriter: 2morrow ok? I'm
exhausted. Goodnite,
everyone

❁

Dear Anna and Joline,

*I am sorry I wrongly accused you of writing that note
about Marty on the website and playing a trick on us.
I was truly upset about losing Marty. I just assumed it
was you two. Sorry again.*
Sincerely,
Charlotte Ramsey

Dear Anna and Joline,

*Since you two have a track record of being mean and
nasty, I figured you wrote the note. Sorry.*
From,
Avery

PART TWO

CRAZY SOX

CHAPTER 13

CR

LUCKY NUMBERS

THE GIRLS STARED at the answering machine in disbelief. Maeve clapped her hands and turning to Avery, Isabel, and Charlotte—eyes bright, asked, "Can you believe it? I absolutely have to celebrate!"

Charlotte, her arms folded, glared suspiciously at the machine. "What is that expression ... don't count your chickens before they're hatched? After our wild goose chase out to the empty lot, I'm not sure that's such a great idea. We don't want to be the victims of any more sick jokes!" she replied.

Maeve looked at Charlotte like she was crazy. "This is totally different! Marty's found! He's not lost any more!" She threw up her hands in a cheer.

"Charlotte, maybe you better play the message again so we can write down the number?" asked Isabel.

"Absolutely." Charlotte had already pulled a pad of paper and pencil from her backpack.

"I'll go to the kitchen and see what's in the fridge for an impromptu party. Oh, I wish Katani were here!" Maeve danced her way out of the room.

"Maeve! Stop right where you are!" Avery commanded.

"What is your problem?" Maeve asked. "Didn't you hear? Marty's found! The guy on the phone has our little Marty!"

"That's not why he called us, Maeve! Didn't *you* hear what he said?" Avery gulped before she could get out the last words. "He wants to keep *our* Marty."

"Ohhh." Maeve was shocked. Her face fell. She had been so excited she had missed that part of the message.

"Are you sure, Avery?" Isabel asked.

"I'm positive. He said he didn't want the reward, remember? He said he wants to pay us money to keep Marty."

"We can't do that," Charlotte said in a firm voice. "Marty belongs with us!"

"Listen to the message again." Avery gestured to the machine. "He wants to keep Marty."

The four girls gathered around the answering machine. Charlotte couldn't believe that something so small contained such vital information. She took a deep breath and pushed the play button.

"Hello. I want you to know your dog ... your little dog ... is OK. No worry. He is safe. He no hurt." The girls looked at each other. Maeve clasped her hand to her heart and smiled with relief.

"Wait! Listen to this next part ..."

"I no want reward. I pay you a hundred times that amount to keep the dog. Call me at 555-0147."

Avery folded her arms across her chest. "I told you," she said to her friends. This was one contest that Avery wished she hadn't won.

Maeve frowned. "No! That can't be right. He must not know what he was saying. Why would he pay to keep Marty ... why, that is simply ... simply ..."

"True!" Isabel retorted.

"Well, of course Marty's a star," Maeve exclaimed indignantly. "But you don't think he seriously means to keep him, do you?"

Avery shrugged. "He sounded pretty serious to me."

"Come on, Maeve—think about it. He said he would pay a hundred times the amount of our reward to keep Marty. What's a hundred times one hundred dollars?" Isabel asked.

Charlotte quickly calculated the sum in her head. "Ten thousand dollars," she said quietly.

"Oh, my gosh!" Isabel gasped in disbelief.

"Seriously! Who would actually pay $10,000 for a mutt?" Maeve asked.

"Somebody with a whole lot of money," Charlotte replied.

For her part, Avery looked stung. "Marty isn't just any old dog, Maeve."

"It's true," murmured Charlotte. "Marty is really, really something special."

"But you guys, it's ten thousand dollars," Maeve argued. "Do you know what you can buy with $10,000?"

"A car," Isabel said.

"A trip to Europe," added Charlotte.

"Marty," Avery decided.

"What if it's a joke?" Isabel wondered. "Maybe Anna and Joline are up to their old tricks again. You know, get back at you and Avery for embarrassing them."

Charlotte shook her head. "It sounds like an adult, not a kid. Let's listen again."

The four huddled closer to the answering machine and Charlotte hit the button one last time.

Maeve shut her eyes and tried to listen harder. "He's hard to understand. He really doesn't speak English very well."

"You're right, Maeve," Isabel said. "This man's first language is definitely Spanish."

"Spanish," Avery was very interested. "Are you positive?"

"Hello ... Mexican heritage here." Isabel was definite.

"OK, so a Hispanic man has Marty and wants to pay us $10,000. Is that what we think?" Maeve asked.

"Wait a minute!" Isabel cried. "You guys, check this out." She held up a flier. "Charlotte, remember when your dad made you redo this because he didn't want you to have your phone number and email address plastered all over Brookline?"

"That's right!" Charlotte had forgotten about that.

"So if this is truly someone you don't know, how did this guy get your phone number?" Isabel asked.

The four were silent as they tried to figure out how some random individual with a lot of money managed to find out Charlotte's phone number.

"It must be Anna and Joline. We are being scammed," Isabel said.

"No, Anna and Joline wouldn't be that obvious after our little 'altercation,'" grinned Avery.

"Do you think any of the original fliers got mixed up with the new fliers, Charlotte?" Maeve asked.

Charlotte disappeared into her bedroom and came out with a handful of fliers. "These were in the garbage can. Do you remember how many we printed off, Isabel?"

"I'm pretty sure we printed off ten."

Charlotte counted the stack of fliers in her hand. "Ten," she said.

"The Queens of Mean are such snakes!" Maeve was fuming. "I believe they would actually find someone to call us and leave a fake message!"

"Come on! Let's not jump to conclusions. Remember

what Ms. Rodriquez said about making accusations. We need to be sure," Charlotte cautioned.

"Wait a minute!" exclaimed an excited Avery. "I need to show you all something." She reached into her worn blue backpack, fumbled around and pulled out the newspaper from lunch. Maeve grimaced when she saw the sticky mess.

"Is there jelly on that thing?"

Avery ignored her and uncrumpled the wadded-up mess of sticky paper (and jelly) and spread it on the floor. "Check this out," she said proudly as she pointed to a blurry photograph of the Red Sox dugout.

Isabel, Maeve and Charlotte looked at each other. Was Avery losing her mind, wondered Charlotte. What did that picture of the Red Sox dugout have to do with Marty?

"Look!" an agitated Avery tapped on the corner of the picture. "Can't you see who this is?" The girls bent down. It was Isabel who saw it first—two familiar shapes in the corner. She looked up. "Avery, is that who I think it is?"

"OH! It's him. It's really Marty and Happy Lucky Thingy is with him." Maeve was beside herself with excitement.

Isabel scrutinized the picture again. "Avery, I think it could be him."

Charlotte wasn't convinced. "I know it looks a lot like Marty, but I'm not jumping to any more conclusions without really good evidence." And after all that had happened she was firm on that. No more *faux pas*, as Sophie would say.

The BSG marched up to the Tower. Charlotte sat on her window seat and stared out into the growing darkness as lights blinked on in the city. She only half listened as Isabel wrote down ideas from Avery and Maeve on one of Katani's dry erase boards. She wondered about the mysterious voice on the phone. What if someone had really found Marty? Of course, the outrageous reward made her suspect Anna and Joline. But after what Ms. Rodriguez said to her today, she knew she had to be super careful about accusing the Queens of Mean again.

Ms. Rodriguez had reminded her that, as a budding journalist, she should depend on her powers of observation. Charlotte grabbed her reporter's notebook and looked at the notes she had scribbled shortly after Marty ran off.

The Disappearance

- *dashed off without leash*
- *no collar*
- *nothing on him—EXCEPT Happy Lucky Thingy!*

Suddenly, Charlotte jumped up. Why *hadn't* she thought of this before?

"Everyone!" Charlotte exclaimed, delighted with her sudden epiphany.

"What?" Avery asked.

"Happy Lucky! When Marty ran off, he had Happy Lucky in his mouth."

"Yeah? So?" Avery asked.

"So I wrote my phone number on the little white tag. You know, the tag on the side of Happy Lucky."

"You did?" Isabel was impressed her friend had been so responsible. That was Charlotte, Isabel smiled. Always thinking. She would definitely go to Europe with Charlotte when they were older.

Charlotte looked at her friends with wide eyes. "You know what that means?"

The girls were afraid that if they said the words out loud they would jinx it. Finally Maeve murmured, "The call might be for real?"

Charlotte grinned. "Bingo!"

The four scrambled down the ladder stairs and rushed toward the telephone.

Charlotte hit the button and they listened intently to the message one more time.

"How can we tell for sure if we're being scammed or not?" Maeve asked.

Charlotte thought about how to get out of that pickle. "What if we asked him where he got the phone number from? Then if he says from the tag on Happy Lucky Thingy we'll know that this is the real deal."

"Let's do it!" Avery enthused. She picked up the phone and shoved it toward Charlotte. "Can we call him now?"

"I don't know … Shouldn't we wait and ask my dad first?"

Avery hesitated, "Well, after this morning I'd say yes, but this is sorta an emergency. We don't know for sure if Marty is OK and the sooner we call, the sooner we get him back! And … we're safe at home. We're not going to any dumpster in a strange neighborhood, or giving out our address."

Charlotte considered this. She didn't want to get in any more trouble. "Well, I guess we could just call him and check, and we can always just hang up if he's weird or something." She began to dial.

"Wait!" Isabel said. "If this guy speaks Spanish, why don't I call? It would make things easier. That way I could ask him if he was serious about the reward thing."

Charlotte handed the phone to Isabel and she punched out the numbers.

"Voicemail," she whispered.

Isabel rattled off something in Spanish.

"What did you say?" Charlotte asked.

"I told him that I was calling about the dog and that he could call me at my home number. I told him to ask for Isabel."

"What about the reward? Did you say anything about the reward?" Avery asked.

"No, but when he calls, I'll tell him that we have to have the dog back. That we are too sad without him."

"This is so fabulosity! Maybe he'll call tonight. Isabel can make plans for the exchange. And then it really will be time to celebrate!" Maeve began to do a happy dance, making her friends giggle.

"Yeah, let's celebrate tomorrow night, once we get Marty back. Then Katani can be here too," Avery suggested.

"Yuri promised me that he was saving a special bone for when Marty returned. I'll pick that up as a little welcome home present," Charlotte said, her voice catching. Was she getting too excited over nothing again? She crossed her fingers behind her back. *Please, let it be true*, she whispered to herself.

"Ooh! I really want to be in charge of his welcome home outfit!" Maeve begged. "I saw a really cute dog sweater at Ms. Pink's on Harvard Street, and it's starting to get cold. With Marty's short fur, I think a little sweater would help keep him warm. Besides, he'll look so cute!"

Charlotte and Isabel clapped their hands in agreement, but Avery looked completely horrified. "Aw, geesh, Maeve.

Are you serious? I always laugh when I see animals dressed like people. Besides, Marty is a manly dog. He doesn't need some fancy-shmancy little sweater to keep him warm," Avery argued.

Maeve grinned mischievously. "We'll see," she replied.

OUT TO PASTURE

Big Blue lurched to a stop in the dirt parking lot of High Hopes Riding Stable. Katani couldn't wait to see Penelope again—she burst out of the car the moment Grandma Ruby put on the breaks and came to a complete stop. Kelley trailed after her.

Katani took a long look around at the barn and rolling meadows surrounding her. She was so far from the traffic and the crowded city sidewalks that this place seemed like her own special world. Unlike the last time, she couldn't wait to smell the grass, the trees, and the horses. She saw Penelope trotting around the corral by herself and ran to step on the bottom board of the fence to get a better view. When Katani made the clucking noise with her tongue, Penelope lifted her head up, turned toward her, and trotted over.

It was hard to believe that this was only their third lesson. Katani felt a connection with Penelope that she couldn't describe, as though she had known the horse for her whole life. Katani was certain the feeling was mutual, as Penelope lifted her head over the top of the fence and nuzzled her shoulder.

On the way home from school, Kelley and Katani had stopped at Yuri's vegetable stand and bought two apples. Katani held her hand out and offered an apple to Penelope.

"Make sure you keep your hand flat," Claudia reminded her. "Horses can't see what's in front of their mouths. You don't want her to accidentally bite you."

Penelope's soft lips wrapped around the apple. She took a bite into the fruit, splattering juice and tiny bits of apple all over Katani and Kelley.

"Oooo!" Kelley said. "Penelope is a very messy eater."

"She eats like a horse," Katani laughed.

Kelley looked frantically about. "I want to feed my horse, too. Where's Wilbur? Wilbur!" Kelley called.

"Come on, let's go find him," Katani said. She grabbed Kelley's hand and together they ran toward the stable.

On Wednesday, the girls had learned the names of the tack, the equipment that goes on a horse. Today they were learning how to saddle the horses.

"Don't worry, we'll continue to help you until we're a hundred percent certain you can do it on your own," Claudia reassured both of them. Claudia was Katani's kind of girl. She had a take-charge attitude; she expected that people would rise to the challenge, but she gave them a ton of support to do it. Katani admired the cute little instructor very much. She was going to record some of Claudia's motivational techniques in her notebook at home. Maybe she could use them for her own fashion and advice empire someday.

Katani curried Penelope all by herself today. Although Claudia did most of the hoof picking thing, she gave Katani her first lesson. She instructed her to pick up Penelope's hoof. "You stand like this and tap on her leg. She likes to have her hoofs picked, so she's more than willing to pick up her foot for you. You just gotta be careful that when she puts her hoof down she doesn't put it down on *your* foot. I've had that happen more often than I'd care to remember. Believe me— it's not pleasant!" Penelope was her usual polite self. Claudia told Katani that Penelope and Wilbur were her two favorite horses. They were gentle and friendly and liked people—the perfect horses for beginning riders.

Katani couldn't wait to get in the saddle. She remembered to swing her leg slowly over Penelope and to pat her on the neck. Once she was settled comfortably on Penelope's back, Claudia gave her the go-ahead to head to the ring. Katani gave Penelope a gentle kick and off they went, Kelley following close behind her on Wilbur. Claudia led Wilbur herself, however. Samantha and Catherine ran on the ground alongside Kelley. The huge smile on Kelley's face told Katani that her sister was enjoying the experience too. At one point, Kelley forgot herself and dropping her reins, threw up her hands in the air and yelled, *"Wilbur Loves Me!"* Claudia had to stop Wilbur and gently encourage Kelley to collect herself, which to Katani's surprise, she did readily. Katani was impressed. Maybe this hippotherapy would really help her sister.

Katani couldn't remember a time when Kelley was happier. At school, Kelley was having an easier time concentrating with her special tutors. Even at home, she seemed more relaxed, handling the bright colors and music better than before. Katani suspected that the riding lessons were the reason for these changes.

Katani reached down and gave Penelope another pat before she encouraged her to trot on. Maybe there was a little magic in riding. Katani always felt in charge—that was her nature—but she wasn't always relaxed. Around Penelope, she felt both in charge and relaxed. This was definitely a new and pleasurable experience for her.

When the sisters' lesson was over, Claudia told Samantha and Catherine to take Kelley back to the stable. "I want a few minutes to go over some things with Katani," she explained.

Claudia proceeded to give Katani a few new pointers on the proper techniques for *posting*—moving up and down in the saddle to match the rhythm of the horse's trot. Katani soaked up the advice like a sponge and rode around the ring a few times using her new technique.

"Great job, Katani," Claudia clapped. "I'm really impressed. I hope your parents will think about getting you some private lessons. You have real talent," she said as Katani dismounted Penelope.

Katani felt like she might burst with pride. For the first time in her life, she was good at something "athletic." Until last week she had never thought of horseback riding as an actual sport. But the day after Katani's first lesson, every muscle in her body was aching. There was pain in muscles she didn't even know she had. She concluded that if this wasn't athletic, then she didn't know what *was*. She pulled a carrot out of her pants pocket and gave it to Penelope. She thought her animal friend needed a reward too.

When Grandma Ruby came back to pick up the girls, Claudia filled her in on their lesson. "And this one," she said, nodding toward Katani, "should be encouraged to take more lessons. She is catching on quickly."

Mrs. Fields asked Katani to take her sister to the car. Kelley was tired after her lesson and Mrs. Fields wanted everything to stay on a positive note. "I found a lovely bakery in Weston Center and bought a couple of cookies for you girls."

Kelley jumped up and twirled around. "Love those cookies," she exclaimed. Even Claudia laughed. Kelley was just so darn funny sometimes, Katani thought as she smiled at her sister.

As the sisters headed back to Big Blue, Claudia turned to face Mrs. Fields. The petite instructor straightened her shoulders and said, "Unfortunately, I have some disappointing news to report. I'm afraid the sessions will have to end at the end of next month. We lost a major funding source and that impacts our deadline to begin repairs to the stable. Unless we find additional funds between now and then, I think we might be out of business."

"Oh, my," Grandma Ruby exclaimed with dismay.

"Our volunteers have been hoping that a financial angel will swoop down and save the stable at the last minute," Claudia added.

From the car, Katani strained her ears to hear what Claudia was saying.

She overheard Claudia talking about how the necessary repairs to bring the stable up to health department codes would come to thousands of dollars. If the money didn't come and come soon, High Hopes would be forced to stop lessons and move the horses to another facility. Katani knew that the other facility was simply too far away. These lessons had quickly become an unexpected gift to Katani and Kelley. She hoped she wouldn't have to give it up, but how in the world could she find that kind of money to save the stable?

Kgirl

Kgirl List:

What I'd love to have for riding lessons (if I could still take them)

1. *Riding pants ... the real kind, not jeans*
2. *White T-with a scooped neck*
3. *My own riding helmet*
4. *Riding boots*
5. *Warm socks*
6. *Money for High Hopes-lots of it!*

CHAPTER 14

ෆ

LUCKY FOR WHO?

"ISABEL! WAKE UP," Aunt Lourdes called from the door. "You have a phone call."

Aunt Lourdes' stern look told Isabel that this was more than just a phone call.

"Who is it?" Isabel asked.

"It's a man!" Aunt Lourdes handed Isabel a robe, as if the man were actually standing in the living room right now. "Why would a man call a 12-year-old girl? And at this hour? You are not in trouble at school, are you?" Aunt Lourdes asked. She looked crossly at Isabel as if it were her fault.

Then a light bulb clicked in Isabel's sleepy brain. "Oh, no, Auntie. It's OK. This is probably the man who said he found Marty. Remember I told you about him?"

"You just don't hand out your phone number to anyone, and I don't care if he is a Red Sox player."

Isabel held up one finger. She needed to take this phone call, and pronto. "I will explain everything as soon as I'm done. I promise," she whispered.

"It is not right. A man talking to a child. You may take

the call, but I will be listening on the extension downstairs."

Isabel understood. She took the phone and gave her aunt a thumbs-up sign.

"Hola?" she said and proceeded to talk with the man in fluent Spanish.

"Isabel?"

"Si. Are you the man who found our dog? Marty?"

"Yes. Yes. Let me explain about the dog."

Isabel remembered Charlotte's plan about figuring out whether or not this guy was telling the truth. "Wait. First I need to know how you got my friend's phone number."

"What?"

"Well, the phone number isn't listed anywhere. Not on the signs. Not on the website," Isabel said. She hoped her aunt was listening so she would know that they had been careful about handing out their phone number.

"Oh, si! The number was on the tag of the pink thing in his mouth."

"Happy Lucky Thingy?"

"You call it what?"

"Happy Lucky Thingy."

The man on the other end began to laugh. "Happy Lucky Thingy? That is a very good good-luck name."

Isabel laughed, too. She couldn't disagree. Happy Lucky Thingy belonged to Avery when she was a baby. She knew it was the only thing Avery had when she arrived in the United States from Korea. Isabel knew how precious it was to Avery. She also knew how precious Marty was to Avery, considering she had given him her special toy to slobber all over.

"So now do you want to talk about the little pooch?" the man asked. That is when the reality set in. The little pooch was Marty! This was the real deal. It wasn't some mean kid hoax like the stuffed animal on the dumpster. But she was definitely not expecting the next thing he had to say.

"My name is Robbie Flores."

Isabel coughed. "Excuse me?" Though she had only moved to Boston a short time ago, she had heard that name often enough to immediately recognize it. Her knees began to shake. This person, this man on the phone, was claiming to be Robbie Flores, the Red Sox rookie that everyone at school was so excited about! She could not believe it. Avery was right. Marty was with the Red Sox. Wait 'til Avery found out which player. Aunt Lourdes gasped on the other end. Robbie Flores was an icon in Boston.

She figured he understood why she was so shocked because she could hear him laugh again. "*Si*. Robbie Flores," he repeated. "I promise you this is true."

"Robbie Flores? As in, the baseball player Robbie Flores?"

"*Si*."

"And *you* have our dog?"

"*Si*. That is what I'm trying to tell you, *señorita!*" Robbie said and then he explained how he found Marty in the parking lot near the festival with no leash or collar on Saturday. He decided that it was unsafe for such a little dog to be running around. Afraid for the puppy's safety, he put the little guy in the car. "Your little dog was very polite and friendly."

Robbie was on his way to the ballpark, but he planned on bringing the dog to the shelter as soon as he got up the next day. So the dog was in the dugout with him for the entire game. Then for the first time in weeks, he came out of his slump. "It was gone. Like it never happened, and I play my best game." Isabel thought that Robbie Flores sounded like a really super chico.

Isabel instantly remembered the picture from the

newspaper. Avery had been sure that that was Happy Lucky in the picture. Avery had been right!

"When I went four for four against the Yankee ace, I began to think that the dog had something to do with it. I named him Lucky Charm, and he has brought me luck, I'm sure of it. So you understand how important it is for me to keep him," Mr. Flores told her.

There was a long pause as if he was waiting for her to reply, but she didn't know what to say. She had been ready for another prank—not for this. Robbie Flores was a whole other story.

"Can you repeat that last part?" she said. Her throat suddenly felt dry.

"He has brought me luck. I want to—no, I really need to keep him."

Isabel sighed. "I'm sorry, Mr. Flores, but you *can't* keep him. Marty is our pet. We don't want to give him away."

"Don't worry, *señorita*. I will pay for the dog."

"How much?" Isabel heard her aunt ask on the extension.

"I have given much thought to this. Lucky Charm is very important to me. I need this dog. I will pay $10,000 to keep Lucky Charm."

"Ten THOUSAND dollars?" Aunt Lourdes was shocked.

Isabel couldn't believe her ears. She had assumed that when the man on the answering machine had said a hundred times as much to keep him, he was just exaggerating to show how much he liked the dog.

"Yes. Ten thousand dollars. I have the check in my hand. I just need to know who to make it out to. I will send it in the mail right away."

Isabel's heart was racing. "No!" she cried. "I'm sorry, Mr. Flores, but the dog is not mine and I don't think he's for sale.

I'll talk to my friends if you want, but that's the best I can do."

"OK. Would you tell them that the Red Sox are depending on Lucky Charm?" Robbie Flores asked.

"I will," she promised.

"Wait, I have an idea! How about you and your friend come to the game this afternoon and I can pay you in person? I'll leave a ticket for you and your friend to pick up."

"Actually … there are five of us." Isabel bit her lip. Another gasp from Aunt Lourdes.

"OK, five tickets. Tickets—not important. What is important is Lucky Charm. He is such a good little dude."

Aunt Lourdes slammed down the phone and Isabel heard her shuffling about. She was coming up the stairs. Isabel pinched herself in disbelief. Was this guy for real?

"OK, Mr. Flores. We'll try to come today,"

"No, no no!" her aunt said, appearing in the doorway. "You five girls are *not* going to meet some crazy person by yourselves, and I can't go with you today. I have to work at the hospital."

"*Si*. I understand, Auntie. But I think it's really Robbie Flores. Maybe Mr. Ramsey could go." Isabel said. She spoke into the phone again and explained, "My aunt won't let me go without adult supervision."

"Then I'll get you six tickets," Robbie Flores agreed. "After the game, meet me by the Clubhouse entrance by Gate A. I'll tell Joe that you're coming to meet me, he'll be at the door." And before she could say another word, Mr. Flores hung up.

"This is ridiculous!" Aunt Lourdes looked troubled. "$10,000 for a dog? Because he thinks it is a lucky charm? He is *loco*. A mad man. I do not approve of this meeting," Aunt Lourdes said. "Not one little bit."

"But Auntie, we get free baseball tickets for today's

game! And if Mr. Ramsey comes with us, we'll be totally fine. Besides, he'll be able to help us make the right decision," Isabel said.

"If it is true, you would be fools not to take the money. You say that Marty belongs to all of you? Then that's two thousand dollars apiece. Just imagine how helpful $2,000 would be …" Her aunt's voice trailed off, but Isabel knew exactly what she was getting at—Isabel's mother's multiple sclerosis. Isabel and her mother and sister had moved from Michigan to Boston, where her Aunt Lourdes lived, since Boston had exceptional hospitals. With all of her mother's medical bills, $2,000 would be very helpful indeed.

Isabel had always thought of Marty as Charlotte's dog because he lived with Charlotte. But they were always saying how Marty belonged to everyone. If that was true, then perhaps her aunt was right. Two thousand dollars for each of them. Not only would that help with the medical bills, but it could pay for lots of airline tickets. Then perhaps her father could visit them for both Thanksgiving *and* Christmas. But, Marty was so loved, especially by Charlotte and Avery. This was going to be one *horrible decision*; Isabel could feel it in her bones.

With a heavy heart, Isabel rushed to the computer to IM the other BSG. What would they think of all of this? She knew they would all be excited about going to a Red Sox game, but Robbie Flores' plea to keep Marty was going to create a terrible dilemma.

File Edit People View Help

4kicks: What up, art girl?
skywriter: Did you talk to
the man? Does he have Marty?
lafrida: I talked to the
guy. u r right. Marty was in
the dugout
4kicks: Wow! ... told ya!!!
skywriter: did he know about
happy lucky thingy?
lafrida: yup
flikchic: who is he?
lafrida: u r not gonna
believe this. robbie flores
has marty.
4kicks: whoooaa ... brb, I
have to jump on my bed!
flikchic: get out
skywriter: r u really sure?
lafrida: positive
4kicks: cool beans!!!
marty's a star
skywriter: when do we get
him back
lafrida: he gave us tickets
for today's game
4kicks: outta sight
lafrida: also a ticket for
your dad, Charlotte. Can he
come?

4 people here
4kicks
skywriter
lafrida
flikchic

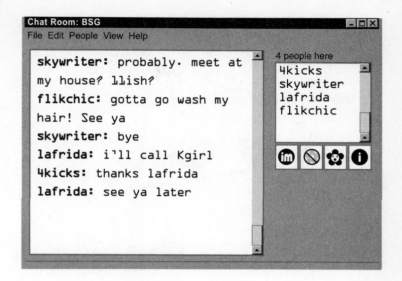

Isabel was glad no one asked anything about the $10,000 reward. She didn't want to put a damper on the idea that they could get Marty back.

Avery's Blog

Top five things to take to a baseball game:

Number 5:   Red Sox Hat
Number 4:   A Red Sox t-shirt or baseball jersey
Number 3:   Money for a Fenway Frank WITH MUSTARD
Number 2:   Pencil for keeping the box score
Number 1:   A baseball glove. How else are you going to
*   catch that homerun or foul ball?*

P.S. Dudes, Marty's been hiding out with a Red Sox player who shall remain nameless ... how cool is that.

CHAPTER 15

☙

GAME FACE

AVERY PULLED on her favorite Red Sox sweatshirt, baseball cap, and grabbed her glove. She couldn't believe their luck—they'd found Marty AND landed tickets for today's game! She couldn't wait until school on Monday! Pete and Dillon would be so jealous when they found out that not only was she at Saturday's game, but she also got to meet Robbie Flores! That alone was exciting enough, but the fact that they had just found Marty was unbelievable! "UNBELIEVABLE!" Avery shouted.

Carla, the Maddens' housekeeper, peeked in the door. "You OK, Avery?"

"No, Carla, I'm not just OK. I'm great! Fantastic! Wonderful! Fabulous! I'm going to the baseball game this afternoon and I'm getting Marty back," Avery said, dancing joyfully around Carla.

"Marty?" Carla asked.

"Marty is my dog ... you know, the BSG dog. Remember, he belongs to all of us, kind of. But if Mom wasn't allergic, he'd be mine. ALL MINE!" Avery jumped up on her bed. The

❁

excitement of Robbie Flores, the Red Sox, and Marty was just too much for her.

"Yes, Marty," Carla said quietly, glancing at the mini zoo Avery had started in her bedroom. So far, it was only a toad and a snake. "Dog is better than snake," Carla said decidedly. She went back to dusting the bookcases in the hallway, leaving Avery to jump off some of her energy. She'd ask Avery to help her clean another day, Carla figured. The little girl was too excited at the moment about finding her dog.

Avery grabbed her baseball mitt and headed to Charlotte's house. She was the first of the BSG to arrive.

"What's that for?" Charlotte asked when she saw Avery's mitt. "I thought we were going to watch a baseball game, not *play* a baseball game."

Avery pounded her fist into the worn-out glove. "Are you kidding me? You gotta bring a baseball mitt to games to catch fouls, or better yet—a homerun ball, depending on where you are sitting of course. Wouldn't it be great if we were seated in the outfield and caught a homer? Wow! What if it was a Robbie Flores homer? And then when we met him and got Marty back, I could have him autograph the homerun ball. Wow! That'd be incredible!" Avery held the glove in the air and pretended to catch a homerun ball. She was completely charged up.

"Now you're sure they're going to have six tickets waiting at the ticket office?" Mr. Ramsey asked.

"That's what Isabel said," Charlotte assured him.

Mr. Ramsey grinned. He looked almost as excited as Avery. "This is unbelievable! I was hoping I'd be able to get to a game this season. I loved going to Red Sox games when I was growing up. I've been so busy these last few years that it's been kinda hard to follow them," Mr. Ramsey said. "You wouldn't believe how many Red Sox fans there were in Paris,

Avery. Actually, I've run into Sox fans everywhere I've traveled. I even met a mountain climber in Nepal who was a Sox fan from Vermont!"

"My dad still follows the team even though he lives in Colorado," said Avery. "I guess people are Red Sox fans for life, even if they move across the country or around the world. Oh look, the pre-game show's on!"

Charlotte and her dad turned their attention to the TV.

"Look!" Avery shouted, pointing to the graphic on the bottom of the screen. She read the caption aloud: "Next up— an interview with Robbie Flores. This is so cool!"

"What's going on?" Katani called up from the foyer.

"Avery, we could hear you from the street," Maeve said.

Avery ran to the banister and looked down at Katani and Maeve. "Hurry up you guys! They're going to interview Robbie Flores on TV. Maybe he'll say something about Marty."

"Or he'll talk about his four-game hitting streak," Katani said when she reached the top step.

Everyone stared at Katani, surprised that she would rattle off a baseball stat like that.

"What?" asked Katani. "I read it in the paper! It's the biggest story in town."

When the pre-game show came back on, there was Robbie Flores sitting on a bench in the locker room. And to everyone's surprise, who should be sitting snugly in his arms, but Marty, the little dude himself. The girls couldn't believe their eyes. The room was silent for a couple of seconds, and then everyone started talking at once.

Charlotte jostled Mr. Ramsey's arm. "Marty!" she cried. "Look, Dad. It's really Marty!"

"I can't believe it," Maeve said.

"This is weird," Katani said. "*Very* weird."

"I told you guys. I TOLD YOU!" said an excited Avery. "Now quiet. QUIET!!! I want to hear what he has to say."

Robbie Flores was in the middle of his interview by the time everyone calmed down. It was a little hard to understand his English. Everyone leaned toward the TV as if being closer to the set would help them make sense of what he was saying.

"This little dude turned it all around for me," Robbie Flores said. "He's my lucky charm."

The camera panned in close on Marty's little face. He was panting under the hot lights. Robbie Flores held up one of Marty's paws and helped him wave at the camera. He seemed to be really stuck on their little dog.

"It looks like he took really good care of him," Katani stared at the screen. "He looks like his well-fed self."

"And check out his collar—it looks like it has rhinestones on it," Maeve was clearly impressed.

"Uh-oh," Charlotte said nervously. "I have a funny feeling about this."

"About what?" Avery asked.

"I mean, if he thinks Marty is his lucky charm, maybe he won't want to give him back," Charlotte said.

A look of horror struck Avery's face. "But he has to give him back! Marty doesn't belong to him," she protested.

"Avery, *you're* the one who noticed that the message on the machine said he would pay us to keep him," Charlotte pointed out.

"Yeah, so?" Avery said. "You heard him on the TV. He doesn't speak English very well. Maybe he was confused and got the words all mixed up."

"His English really isn't that bad," Katani said. "I think Charlotte might be right."

"His English is excellent," Charlotte stated.

Avery pounded her mitt as she spoke. "Listen, he wouldn't have invited us to the game if he didn't plan on *giving Marty back to us.* Isabel didn't say anything about him paying us. You guys are just worrywarts."

The girls nodded half-heartedly. They were all hoping that Avery was right.

HOT SEATS!

"Hey, what kind of seats do you think we'll get?" Charlotte asked, hoping to turn the conversation in another direction.

"I want to be in the outfield so I can catch a home run!" Avery said.

"He's got connections," Katani noted. "Maybe we'll be sitting in box seats."

"Ooh! I didn't even think of that! Maybe we'll get *skybox* seats," Maeve said as she twirled around.

Katani pulled something out of her bag. It was a stuffed animal—a tiny purple pony. "I made a new toy for the little guy," Katani said. "I felt ... inspired." She had sewn it together last night, but the design was Kelley's idea.

"I brought some doggie treats," Avery said, taking the bag from her pocket.

Charlotte pulled a bigger plastic bag from her canvas tote. "I went to see Yuri this morning, and I picked up that bone he's been saving for Marty."

"Hope the ushers don't search us," Katani said. "They'll think we're crazy!"

The doorbell rang and Charlotte ran downstairs to let Isabel in.

"There she is!" Katani said as Isabel jogged up the stairs.

"I was starting to get worried."

"Our bilingual hero," Maeve said, patting Isabel on the back. "I wish I could speak Spanish."

"So what did he sound like?" Avery asked.

"Who?" Isabel asked.

The girls all replied at once, "Robbie Flores!"

"Oh … he was very nice," Isabel said.

"Wow, I can't believe how cool you are about the whole thing," Maeve said. "I mean, if I got to speak to Robbie Flores … well … I'd probably swoon or something." Maeve fanned herself with her hand like a dehydrated Southern belle.

"I hope not, Maeve. That would be totally embarrassing," Avery said, rolling her eyes.

Maeve ignored Avery's comment. She was worried about Isabel. She didn't seem very excited about the game, getting Marty back, or even meeting Robbie Flores in person.

"By the way," Avery said, elbowing Isabel, "Guess who we just saw on TV?"

"Who?" asked Isabel.

"Robbie Flores *and* Marty."

"He went on TV with Marty? Why? What'd he say?" Isabel asked nervously.

"He said something about Marty being the reason for him hitting so well," Charlotte said.

"Yeah, it turns out that Marty is his *lucky charm*," Avery reported.

"I have a bad feeling about this," Charlotte said. "Isabel, did he say anything to you about the reward when you talked to him?"

"Well …"

"Come on. He said lucky charm but he can't honestly think that Marty is the reason why he's playing so well, right?" Katani asked.

"I wouldn't be surprised if he did, Katani," Mr. Ramsey said. "Athletes can be extremely superstitious. Baseball players in particular. Wade Boggs used to eat chicken before every game."

"Didn't he ever get sick of chicken?" asked Katani.

"Maybe, but he would never break his routine. That would be bad luck," answered Mr. Ramsey.

"And Nomar Garciaparra always wore the same T-shirt under his uniform," Avery said. "And every time he got up to bat, he tapped his toes and adjusted his wristbands the same exact way."

Maeve noticed Isabel shift uneasily in her seat.

"Well, what did Robbie say to you?" Maeve asked.

Isabel twirled the ends of her hair and stared at the ground. When she spoke, her voice was so soft that they could barely hear her. "He wants to pay us ten thousand dollars to keep him."

"What?!?" Avery shrieked.

Charlotte sat down with a thud.

Maeve couldn't believe her ears.

"So you heard right on the answering machine. He wasn't just confused. It wasn't a language barrier thing!" Katani exclaimed, but unlike her friends, she didn't look devastated.

In fact, she was smiling. "It's a miracle. I can't believe this. Grandma Ruby said just this morning not to worry. She said we should trust that the universe will provide us with what we need and … and here it is! She was right!"

"I wouldn't call it a miracle, Katani. Robbie Flores wants to *buy* Marty from us," Avery sighed.

"Well," Katani explained. "The stable that Kelley and I ride at doesn't have enough money to make repairs. Ten thousand dollars would help them stay in operation. I can't believe that Robbie Flores wants to buy Marty for $10,000. And he's a celebrity, so maybe he could help get the word out."

"What are you talking about?" Maeve asked.

"The horse therapy place I've been going to with Kelley. It helps a lot of disabled kids. And it was going to have to close because they needed at least ten thousand dollars. And now, just like that—" Katani snapped her fingers, "—we have $10,000 to keep it up and running. Don't you think that's a miracle?"

"But we're not taking the money," Avery said sternly.

Charlotte seemed dazed. "Are you serious, Katani? You would really give up Marty for ten thousand dollars?" Charlotte asked.

Avery shook her head and sighed, "I'm ashamed of you, young lady."

But Katani wasn't going to give up easily. "You couldn't possibly understand, Avery. You have no idea how hard it is to watch someone you love suffer and not be able to do anything because you don't have the money to help them."

Maeve looked at Isabel, who hung her head. Avery glanced at Charlotte, but they both didn't know what to say. No one could believe that Katani would sell their precious Marty, even if it was for her sister and disabled kids.

"There must be another way you could get the money," Maeve said.

"$10,000?" Katani raised an eyebrow at her friends. "I could always just win the lottery, right? C'mon, ten *thousand* dollars is no chump change, and it could help Kelley and tons of other kids."

"Don't you see that Marty is like part of my family to me?" Charlotte asked.

"A dog is not a sister," Katani said. "First of all you *can't* sell people. But people sell dogs all the time. You know I love Marty, but that money could mean so much for Kelley. Besides there are a lot of puppies out there that need a good home. Can we just consider the option?"

"We're not taking the money and that's final! Marty's not for sale," Avery declared. "To even think about it is ... is ... well ... it's cold and heartless!"

Katani's eyes grew large. "Heartless! Heartless? You're the heartless one. You don't care about my sister at all," she sputtered, and with that, Katani stormed out of the room, ran down the stairs and left, slamming the front door behind her.

"What's going on?" Mr. Ramsey asked when he came back into the room. "Charlotte?"

Charlotte opened her mouth to say something but nothing came out. She tried to blink back tears as she summoned the courage to tell her dad what had happened.

Isabel said nothing, but she thought, *Katani's not the only one who could use that money.* As soon as the thought crossed her mind, she felt guilty. Marty was the BSG mascot. How could they sell him?

CHAPTER 16

൪

EXTRA TICKET

THE ROOM WAS eerily quiet after Katani stomped off. Maeve wanted to break the silence by saying something, but oddly enough she couldn't think of anything to say.

Instead, Mr. Ramsey was the one to finally change the subject. "Hmmm ..." he said as he stroked his beard, "it seems that we have an extra ticket."

"Dad!" Charlotte looked appalled.

"I don't mean to be insensitive here, Charlotte. I'm not happy about the way Katani left. It's just that we do have an extra ticket. It seems a shame to let it go to waste. Anyone have any ideas?"

Everyone was quiet.

"How about asking one of your brothers, Avery?" Mr. Ramsey asked.

"I don't think so. Tim is away at college and Scott has an away soccer game. I could never reach him," Avery said.

"How about your brother, Maeve?" Mr. Ramsey asked.

Maeve was startled. "Sam?"

"Yeah ... why not?"

Maeve didn't know what to say. She didn't think that Mr. Ramsey remembered she had a brother. Now here he was inviting him to the baseball game. She wasn't sure she wanted to baby-sit for her pesky little brother—not when she was meeting Robbie Flores—but she didn't have time to make up an excuse.

"Why don't you call your mom?" Mr. Ramsey suggested, handing Maeve the phone. "They can meet us at the trolley stop in ten minutes."

When Maeve told her mom the news, she could hear Sam whooping and cheering in the background. He sounded so excited, which meant he was going to be *so* annoying. By the time Maeve got off the phone, the others were ready to go, so she threw on her coat and they tromped down the stairs and out the door.

Sam was waiting with Ms. Kaplan at the trolley stop.

"Did you have to wear camouflage?" Maeve asked.

"It's my best camouflage!" Sam said defensively. Maeve rolled her eyes.

"Maeve, here's some spending money for you and your brother." Ms. Kaplan slipped her a wad of folded bills. "Now I want you stay with your sister no matter what and listen to Mr. Ramsey," Ms. Kaplan told Sam.

Ms. Kaplan pulled Maeve aside. "Make sure you hold on tightly to his hand in crowds. You know how he can pull away. It only takes one second for someone to get lost," Ms. Kaplan said.

"I know, I know," Maeve grumbled.

Luckily, the trolley arrived and rattled to a stop. Maeve was relieved to finally break away.

Ms. Kaplan was waving from the sidewalk. "Hold his hand," she mouthed. In case there was any doubt, Ms.

❖

Kaplan pointed to her own hand. Maeve complied, but Sam wasn't too happy about holding hands either. His sweaty palm writhed around in her grip.

"Leave me alone," he whined.

"Hey, Maeve, if you want, I can keep my eye on Sam here," Mr. Ramsey offered. He gave Sam a high five. "Us guys'll stick together, right?"

Sam beamed. "Right!"

Mr. Ramsey bent down and whispered, loud enough for Maeve to hear, "I'm sure glad you could come today. Otherwise I'd be stuck with this crazy bunch of girls."

"No prob." Sam looked pleased with himself.

Mr. Ramsey winked at Maeve and pointed out an open railing for Sam to grab onto. Usually there were a couple of seats to spare, but the T was packed because everyone was heading to the game.

Great, at least I won't have any eight-year-old freak-outs to worry about today, Maeve thought. She was sad that Katani hadn't come, but happy that her little brother was going to have an exciting day.

When they got to Fenway, the group made a beeline for the ticket office. "Wow! Look at these seats," Mr. Ramsey said. "We're almost directly behind the warmup circle. I feel like I have died and gone to Red Sox heaven!"

Mr. Ramsey and Avery were excited about the tickets, but Maeve was more excited. Seeing the dreamy Robbie Flores up at bat was too cool for words.

After the other team's third out in the ninth inning, Mr. Ramsey got up to take Sam to the bathroom. Two Cokes and Maeve's little brother was dancing on one foot.

They had just disappeared up into the stands when Avery freaked out. She grabbed Maeve's arm. "Ouch! What is your problem?" Maeve tried to shake Avery loose but Avery had a death grip on her arm.

"You better run and get your brother and Mr. Ramsey. "Flores is first at bat."

"What if he hits a home run? My dad will be so disappointed," Charlotte stood up on her seat to see if she could catch him before they went through the gate. Too late. They were already gone.

The BSG turned their attention back to the main attraction.

"Ave, why …"

"Be quiet," Avery shushed Maeve.

The first pitch was a ball, the second was a ball, and so was the third.

Flores was angry. He walked away from the mound to conference with the Red Sox manager. He was waving his arms and shouting in Spanish.

"What's he saying Isabel; tell me quick?" Avery pleaded.

"He said this was a setup. He's really angry."

Avery put her head in her hands. Flores was going to be intentionally walked—she just knew it.

Charlotte shook Avery. "Avery, look. He's back up. The pitcher's winding up.

"What did we miss?" Mr. Ramsey asked. Charlotte breathed a huge sigh of relief. Her dad and Sam made it back just in time to see Robbie reach for a wide one and slam it over the Green Monster, Fenway Park's famous wall.

Avery, Sam, Mr. Ramsey, Charlotte, and Isabel stood up on the bench and cheered with the rest of the fans. The stadium was so loud Sam's ears started to ring. He clasped his hands over each ear, but kept yelling, too.

Maeve, on the other hand, stepped out into the aisle and danced up and down the stairs.

The Red Sox had won the game and everyone but Katani had seen the great Robbie Flores slam one over the wall.

C℞

"Shall we go meet Robbie Flores?" asked Mr. Ramsey with a wink and a high five to Sam as they headed out of the bleachers after the game.

Avery looked like she was about to faint.

Isabel, Charlotte, and Maeve grabbed each other and screamed "Yes!" so loudly that Maeve's pink baseball cap fell off her head.

Avery led the way to the clubhouse. They held hands as the large crowd tried to squeeze out of the old park at the same time. It was like a conga line with Avery in the lead winding down the ramp, through the concession stands toward a door with a sign that read "Red Sox Clubhouse." They were surrounded by reporters and Red Sox family members. The BSG shuffled into line.

"Who is that, Avery?" Isabel pointed toward an old man in a Red Sox jacket who seemed to be checking IDs.

"That's Joe. He's the guard at the locker room. He's like famous," said Avery. Two legends in one day. Avery figured that this must be the best day … the best day of her life … ever.

Suddenly, Sam began to squirm.

"Chill out, Sam. This is getting embarrassing and you are driving me crazy!" Maeve commanded. If Sam did anything to embarrass her in front of Robbie Flores, she would die. She kneeled and looked Sam in the eye. "You've got to sit still NOW."

"I can't," Sam whispered.

"Again?" Maeve asked. "Well, you're just going to have to wait."

"I can't!" Sam moaned.

"Don't worry, Maeve," Mr. Ramsey said. "I'll handle this. Let's go, big guy."

Not a minute after Mr. Ramsey and Sam left, the locker room door opened. The girls turned with a start. In walked a tall man in a Red Sox warmup suit. And behind him was Robbie Flores.

Maeve's heart began pounding. He seemed much taller than when he was on the field.

Charlotte was worried. She wished her father was there. What if Robbie Flores wouldn't give Marty back?

Robbie Flores had sparkling brown eyes, and dark, wavy hair. He smiled and Maeve thought she might melt on the spot. Luckily, Sam had left with Mr. Ramsey. He'd probably be all over this guy trying to get his autograph.

Avery went right up to Robbie and slapped his hand. "Great game!" she exclaimed.

At first Maeve was thinking how babyish that seemed until she realized that Avery had actually touched Robbie Flores' hand. Oh, if only she'd thought of doing that!

"Which one is Isabel?" he asked, looking around at all the girls.

Isabel raised her hand, "*Hola, Señor Flores*. I'm Isabel. Nice to meet you."

"You are the owner of the little dog?" Flores asked.

"No, I—" Avery stopped herself. "We all are." She stepped forward and Charlotte followed suit.

"We all take care of Marty, *señor*," Isabel said. "He is our mascot, our pet. He lives with Charlotte though," she added, gesturing toward her friend.

"Thank you all for meeting with me here today," Mr. Flores began. "*Gracias*. Without this dog I'm afraid I would be on a plane back to the minor leagues. Until that day in the park my bat was very quiet. But ever since I found this lucky charm, my bat has come alive. I owe much to him. Much to you for my success."

"Us? You owe much to us?" Maeve asked.

"Oh, yes. My Lucky Charm isn't good just for me. He is good for the Red Sox. He is good for all of Boston," Mr. Flores said, adding, "Lucky Charm gives the fans a reason to cheer."

"You really believe that the Red Sox would lose if it weren't for Marty?" Maeve asked.

"*Si!*"

Charlotte turned to Maeve and gave her a look. She didn't want Maeve making Robbie Flores uncomfortable.

"Mr. Flores, you are a great player. You don't really need a dog to help you," Charlotte said with conviction. She hoped the great Robbie Flores would come to his senses about Marty.

"Look at my record since I found Marty. The numbers will prove that it's true. This little fellow is my lucky charm. And I have to thank you girls for providing me with my little pooch. I promise you will be rewarded."

"Where is Marty?" Avery asked.

"Marty?" Robbie Flores asked.

"The little dog," Isabel explained. "The one you call your lucky charm."

"You call him Marty? It's not the name I expected for such a peppy dog. Better than, what did you say? Happy Lucky Thing? What a name!" Mr. Flores opened the door to the locker room and called something in Spanish. Moments later, a trainer came in carrying a bag.

"Marty!" Avery shouted when she saw the cute mutt's head sticking out.

"Marty!" Charlotte squealed.

Marty squirmed around in the bag.

"Settle down, little one," Mr. Flores commanded. Even though Robbie Flores was a world-class athlete, he wasn't quick enough to keep Marty from bounding out of the bag and jumping around on the floor. He hopped up on his hind legs as he wiggled and shimmied between the girls.

Avery sat down on the floor and in an instant Marty was licking her face. Then Marty saw Charlotte and jumped into her arms.

Charlotte looked like she was about to cry. Marty licked her face and jumped out of her arms. Then he went over to Isabel and danced around her. Isabel laughed as Marty yipped and barked.

Maeve was completely surprised when the little guy jumped into her arms and began to lick off her fruity-floral-scented body lotion.

"Friendly fellow, no?" Mr. Flores asked, watching the happy reunion. Robbie Flores let out a loud whistle. Marty immediately stopped dancing. He scampered back to Mr. Flores and jumped in his bag.

Charlotte and Avery looked at each other. They were both wondering the same thing ... Had Marty forgotten who he belonged to?

"I'm prepared to write you a check for ten thousand dollars right now. Which one of you do I make it out to?"

The girls looked at each other in panic. "Mr. Flores, you don't understand," Charlotte said. "Marty is not for sale. Not for $10,000 ... not for any price." Where was her father? She needed him. Charlotte looked anxiously at the door. He should be back by now.

"No?"

❀

✿

Charlotte glanced at Avery who nodded supportively. "If you wouldn't mind, we'd really like to have our dog back. Here, Marty, come here, boy," she called. Marty looked back and forth between Robbie and Charlotte.

Maeve thought the little dude was being a tad disloyal.

Robbie Flores looked genuinely sad, but he shook head in protest. "No. I'm very sorry, but I can't let you take Lucky Charm now. I have big game on Tuesday and my Lucky Charm must be there. After that, we fly to Baltimore. I need my Lucky Charm there too," Robbie Flores picked up Marty and patted his head. "Think about my offer, girls. It is very fair. I'll call you after the next game. Think about how much your city depends on this little guy right here. I hope you agree to accept my offer." Robbie Flores waved politely and exited through the back door.

The usher led the parade of crestfallen girls out of the room, just as Mr. Ramsey and Sam were returning from the trip to the restroom.

"Dad," Charlotte cried. "Where were you? Robbie Flores was here and he doesn't want to give Marty back!"

Sam tugged eagerly at his sister's hand. "Did you meet him? Did you shake his hand? Did you get his autograph?" Sam asked.

The girls were quiet, but Sam continued to pepper them with questions. "Was he friendly? Did he give you the ball from the game?"

"Remember how I told you to calm down?" asked Maeve.

"Yeah?"

"*Well calm down.*"

"Geesh, OK." Sam put his hands in his pockets and pulled away from Maeve.

"Where's Marty?" Mr. Ramsey asked.

"Robbie Flores wouldn't give him back!" Maeve cried. desperately. "At least not today."

Mr. Ramsey looked confused. "Wait a minute … then why did he have you come down here?" he asked.

"He didn't bring us to the game to give back Marty. He brought us down here to buy him!" Charlotte was distraught. "He wants to keep Marty. *Forever*."

"He thinks he can't play baseball without Marty," explained Isabel.

"He really does want to pay us ten thousand dollars," Maeve said. "Can you believe that? I just can't believe it."

Mr. Ramsey surveyed the girls. Mr. Ramsey knew what extra money would mean to Isabel's family. "What did you all decide?"

"We didn't take the money, of course," Maeve told him.

Charlotte added, "He wanted to write us a check."

Mr. Ramsey considered this. "A check … for $10,000. But you girls didn't take it?"

They all shook their heads.

"Let me get this straight. You didn't take the check, but he didn't return Marty? What's going on here?"

"Dad! Marty is not for sale! We just have to convince Robbie Flores to give him back." Charlotte sighed. "At least we know that Mr. Flores likes Marty …"

"Ten thousand dollars is a lot of money," Mr. Ramsey looked at Isabel again.

"Perhaps we *should* think it over," Isabel said softly.

"What! How can you say that?" Avery exclaimed. "It's Marty. I rescued him from a garbage can. We saved him! He's our dog!"

"I'm not trying to be rude, Avery, but you don't know what it's like to really need money. I mean *really* need it. You live in a nice big house, with a cleaning woman even! And you get money from your parents to buy you anything you want. Where I am from, there just isn't enough money to go around. My mother's medical bills are high and we ..." Isabel trailed off. "Oh ... never mind," she said, looking embarrassed.

Avery didn't know what to say in response to Isabel's outburst. She couldn't help that she lived in a big house. Did that mean she would have to give up a dog she loved? Avery looked at Charlotte. Char looked stricken too.

Maeve understood Isabel's situation, but still, it didn't quite seem fair. "So you think *you* should take the money?"

"We could divide it five ways. Two thousand dollars would go a long way to help with my mother's medical expenses or pay for airline tickets so my father can visit for the holidays."

Mr. Ramsey placed his hand on Charlotte's shoulder. "How about we sleep on this, girls?" The BSG said nothing. As they proceeded out of the ballpark—one father, one tired eight-year-old, and four solemn girls—Charlotte wondered, would any amount of sleep make all five members of the BSG agree with each other?

CHAPTER 17

⋙

DEADLOCKED

"CHARLOTTE, BREAKFAST!" Mr. Ramsey called.

Charlotte groaned and rolled over, pulling the pillow on top of her head. She'd been vaguely aware her dad was up to something in the kitchen. She could hear the clanging of pots and pans and eggs cracking on the countertop. The air was pungent with coffee and bacon.

"I made your favorite—chocolate-chip pancakes. Hurry up, Char, they're going to get cold."

Charlotte didn't want to eat. She didn't want to get out of bed. She had been up all night tossing and turning. She couldn't stop thinking about Marty, the ten thousand dollars, Isabel and her family, and Katani and Kelley's riding stable. Life was so complicated sometimes. She didn't want to lose Marty, but what about Isabel and Kelley? Was it easier for grownups to make these decisions? she wondered.

"Rough night?" Mr. Ramsey asked when Charlotte stumbled into the kitchen.

Charlotte nodded and sat silently at the table, staring blankly at the stack of pancakes in front of her.

They looked yummy, but Charlotte didn't have the heart to tell her dad she wasn't hungry. He drenched the pancakes with syrup and divided them into pizza shaped slices. Instead of eating, however, she just pushed the little triangles around on her plate.

"Do you think I'm mean?" she finally asked.

"Why would you say that?"

Charlotte sighed and placed her fork on the side of her plate. "About wanting to keep Marty and not take the money?"

"No honey. This is an impossible situation. In the end, money doesn't buy what's really important in life, which is love. You love Marty," Mr. Ramsey said, taking a sip of coffee.

"But the money sure seemed important to Isabel and Katani yesterday."

"I know, honey, but $2,000 or even $10,000 isn't going to make Isabel's mother get better … and Kelley will always be autistic," Mr. Ramsey said.

"But would it help?" Charlotte asked.

Mr. Ramsey shrugged. "Of course it would help both of them. But Charlotte, people are always going to need money for a worthwhile cause. What was Katani saying yesterday? Something about a miracle? I don't think anyone would want a child to give up a beloved pet."

Charlotte blinked. She had not forgotten the pre-game quarrel with Katani.

"We can always contact Mr. Flores," Mr. Ramsey told her. "If you believe that bringing Marty home is best, I will stand by you, and we will get him back. I miss the little guy, too."

For the first time since last night, Charlotte felt OK. Marty was in her heart. *Still, everyone in the BSG is important to me*, she thought as she scraped the pancake remains off of her plate and then put it in the dishwasher.

After cleaning up, Charlotte left the kitchen and went up to her room to call Katani.

"Hello, Mrs. Summers? This is Charlotte Ramsey. Is Katani there?"

"I'm sorry, sweetie," Mrs. Summers said. "Katani's not here right now. She's still at the stable with her sister Kelley. Can I take a message?"

"No ... that's OK. I'll call back later," Charlotte promised Mrs. Summers and then hung up the phone.

She was about to crawl back into her bed for the rest of the day and read—reading was her salvation—when suddenly she had an idea. Charlotte picked up the phone one more time and dialed.

When the doorbell rang an hour later, Charlotte dashed to the front door. Maeve Kaplan-Taylor was standing on the steps wearing a lime green jacket and holding a little white bag.

"I stopped by Montoya's and picked up two cherry turnovers," she said as she came in. "I thought that might cheer you up."

Charlotte smiled.

"The only thing I could think of to make you even cheerier is if I had Nick deliver the turnovers in person," Maeve said with a twinkle in her eye.

"Thank goodness you didn't!" Charlotte gasped. "Look at me! I have a severe case of bedhead." Charlotte shook her head to demonstrate to Maeve the mass of cowlicks in her hair. Suddenly a scary thought dawned on her ... "Maeve, you didn't! Tell me he isn't here!"

Maeve chuckled. "No, no, he isn't here," Maeve assured her friend. "But I still think Nick would have done the trick. Come on, let's go to the Tower. Things always look better from up there."

Charlotte brought up two glasses of apple cider and Maeve brought the cherry turnovers.

"By the way, have you talked to Katani?" Charlotte asked as she munched away on her pastry. It was so delicious. Mrs. Montoya should have her own baking show. She was the best baker in the world. Nick had once told her that his mother perfected all the recipes in the shop.

"Actually, I did talk to her for a while online last night," Maeve said.

"Did she tell you what exactly she meant by miracle?"

Maeve licked some gooey cherry off her fingers. "Yes. The health department is making High Hopes repair their stable. The only thing is, the repairs will cost just over $10,000. If they don't get the money by next week they'll have to move to another location. But Katani said it is too far away for her Grandma to drive to. You have to admit that it's pretty ironic, Charlotte," Maeve said.

"What do you mean?"

"Robbie Flores is offering us almost the exact amount that Katani needs. It's just such a weird coincidence," Maeve said.

Then it dawned on Charlotte. "Are you saying that we should give up Marty so Katani's riding program can have the money?"

Maeve shrugged and looked down. "I dunno. Maybe if you heard it from Katani's point of view ..."

Charlotte couldn't believe what she was hearing. "But Maeve, what about my point of view? When I was little I lost my mother. Then in France I lost my cat. I'm just ... I'm just ..." Her lip began to tremble. "I'm just so sick of losing everything I love." Charlotte sniffled back tears. She would not let herself cry again. "Besides, if you love something or someone, you just don't sell it because someone offers you a lot of money. Not if you love it."

"I didn't mean …" Maeve trailed off. "This is so awful, Charlotte. I can see everybody's point of view. Marty should be here, but Isabel and Katani could use the money."

Silence.

"Listen, Charlotte. I love Marty just as much as you do." Charlotte gave her a look.

"What? I do. And I promise that whatever you decide I'll support you. But …"

"But what?"

"Well, when we found Marty we did agree that he belonged to all of us. Maybe the right thing to do is to vote on it."

"Vote? Vote! I think that's an awful idea!" Charlotte cried.

"But Charlotte, it's the only fair way …"

"This is great, just great. Well, I know how Isabel and Katani are going to vote. And by the way you've been talking, I guess I know how you're going to vote too. So that leaves me and Avery. Three to two. I better get used to being petless again."

Charlotte's Journal

I saw Miss Pierce tonight. She says that I must always hope in my heart that things will work out and that Marty will come home. I think Miss Pierce is as attached to Marty as I am. And to think! Just a short time ago I was worried that Miss Pierce would throw Dad and me out of our cozy little place here on Corey Hill…because she didn't like pets! But Marty is so easy to fall in love with … he's one of a kind.

CHAPTER 18

❧

THE BEST AND WORST

"SO HOW WAS your weekend, class?" Ms. Rodriguez asked as the Monday morning bell rang to start homeroom.

Katani's weekend had been partly wonderful, but in a way it was more horrible than she could have imagined.

Yesterday she went riding, and that had been amazing. When Penelope saw Katani standing at the corral, she lifted her head as if to say "What's up, girl?" and nickered softly. Nickering was what Claudia McClelland had called that soft, low horse sound that came from deep inside Penelope. It was different from a whinny, which was louder and shriller. A nicker meant: "Hello! I see you by the fence. How are you?"

But Penelope didn't just nicker. She trotted right over to the fence and nuzzled her velvety nose into Katani's shoulder. She never thought her stable chores, like cleaning out a stall, could be an act of love, but to Penelope, they truly were. The sooner Katani got the stall mucked out, the sooner she could curry Penelope and ride her. Currying was OK, but riding her was the best thing in the whole world. On top of Penelope, Katani felt she could conquer the world. Plus, riding was just so much fun. Her dad always called Katani his serious daughter. Until she met the BSG, Katani had been all work. Now she had friends and Penelope.

Katani suddenly realized that she had completely spaced out on Ms. Rodriguez as Joey Peppertone shouted, "It was the most awesome thing I've ever seen!"

Pete Wexler mimed hitting a ball.

It didn't take long for Katani to figure out they were talking about Saturday's baseball game.

Joey's comment about the Red Sox game reminded her of the other half of her weekend—the horrible half. She remembered that stupid fight before the baseball game. Katani felt bad that she had stormed off in a fit. At the time she just couldn't help herself. The thought that the stable might close seemed so unfair.

The $10,000 that Robbie Flores offered for Marty would mean so much to so many kids at High Hopes, including her sister, not to mention herself. Did she want the money for herself so she could continue to ride Penelope? Katani felt a sudden stab of guilt.

She loved riding so much that maybe she really wanted the stable to stay open for herself. But Katani also knew that as wonderful as riding was for her, it was ten times more important to Kelley.

Why, she couldn't completely understand, but the horses had helped. Katani understood exactly what her sister was going through. On horseback, she wasn't just Katani Summers, the non-athletic one of the family, and her sister wasn't Kelley Summers, the autistic one of the family. They were both something much, much more.

But the offer of $10,000 had changed everything. How could Avery and Charlotte give up such an amazing chance to help so many people? And then there was Marty. Marty was the sixth member of the BSG. Katani shook herself. This was all becoming way too complicated. She had a headache thinking about it all.

Suddenly the class broke out into laughter. Katani snapped out of her thoughts about the weekend. What were they all talking about? What was so funny? She turned to listen to Dillon, super jock.

"Socks! What do you mean he hasn't washed his socks?" Dillon asked Pete.

"Well, you know how superstitious ball players are. Remember the 2004 Red Sox team? A lot of them didn't shave or cut their hair because they were afraid they'd bring on the curse of the Great Bambino," Pete told him.

"What does that have to do with Robbie Flores, though?" Dillon demanded.

"Well, Flores is shaven and it looks like he just got his hair cut. So I was thinking maybe his socks are his lucky charm," Peter suggested. He pulled his socks up over the ends of his pants and pretended to hit a homerun. Then he waved his hand in front of his face and held his nose as if his socks were the stinkiest things he'd ever smelled. The class burst into hysterical laughter.

"Hey, quiet down!" Avery commanded. Everyone stopped laughing immediately.

Katani was shocked. Avery never wanted the laughter to die down when it came to sports talk, especially sports talk about the Red Sox.

"You guys, I know what Robbie Flores' lucky charm is and believe me, it's not a pair of socks."

"Well what is it?" Peter asked.

"It's our dog! Marty!" Avery cried.

Suddenly the room was agog with curious chatter.

Ms. Rodriguez looked skeptical. "The one that's missing? Avery, are you sure?"

"Of course I'm sure! Robbie Flores invited us to the game on Saturday and we got to meet him afterwards."

"*You* got to meet *Robbie Flores*?" Dillon asked. This was the moment Avery had been waiting for.

"Really?" Peter wanted to know.

"Really," Charlotte was right there to back up the claim. "We saw Marty on Saturday. He was there at the game. Robbie keeps him in the dugout."

"Hey! I did see a little dog in the dugout during the game! Jerry Remy and the other announcers were talking about the dog," Pete said. "That's really Marty?"

Avery nodded. "Flores thinks he's out of his slump because he found Marty and now he doesn't want to give him back!"

Don't say a word, Katani told herself as she listened to all this. She pretended to act disinterested. But Avery was going on and on, making it sound like Robbie Flores wasn't playing fair because he didn't want to give back Marty. Katani thought of his generous offer, and it all became too much for her to handle.

"First of all, Robbie Flores *didn't* steal Marty," Katani snapped. "He found him running loose in the park with no collar and called when he found a number on Happy Lucky Thingy's tag. He did call, because he wanted us to know that Marty was OK. And now you are making him out to be selfish. Marty is the hero of Boston! And Robbie is willing to pay $10,000 for his 'Lucky Charm' and that money could help a lot of people..." Katani had stood up and raised her voice so the whole class could hear. A hush fell over the room.

"Robbie Flores wants to pay you $10,000 to keep your dog?" Dillon asked.

Avery and Charlotte stared at Katani in disbelief. Was Katani even a BSG anymore? wondered Avery.

Everyone started talking at once and everyone had his or her own opinion.

"OK people, settle down," Ms. Rodriguez motioned as she walked up and down the aisles. "Katani, it seems like you feel pretty strongly about this. Why do you think you girls should accept the money?"

Katani felt everyone's eyes upon her. She tried to summon the confidence she felt while she was on Penelope, remembering what it was like to be on top of her horse and feeling like she was on top of the world.

"A lot of you guys know I have a sister at this school, Kelley. And if you know Kelley, you know that she is ... extraordinary. The reason why Kelley seems different than us is because she's autistic," Katani explained. She couldn't believe she was standing in front of her seventh-grade homeroom talking about Kelley. But this was important, and she needed her classmates to understand why. "Well, Kelley just started a new therapy, horse riding therapy, and it's helping her a lot. Horse riding is good for autistic kids—not just physically, but socially and emotionally, too. You wouldn't believe how much of a difference it has made in just the short time she's been riding."

Everyone in the room was hanging on her every word, even Anna and Joline. Katani took a deep breath and continued. "But last week I learned that the stable, the High Hopes Riding Stable, is going to be shut down. They need to make repairs, which will cost more than ten thousand dollars. There isn't time for a fund-raiser or anything. They need the money now. And then this miracle comes along—Robbie Flores is offering us that exact amount! That money would keep, not just Kelley, but lots of kids like Kelley, learning and improving every day."

Charlotte was sure there was something wrong with that argument, but she just couldn't figure out what it was. Katani had a right to care about her sister, but didn't she care at all about Marty and what he meant to her, Avery, and the BSG? Charlotte wasn't even mad at Katani anymore. She was just confused. She wondered if Katani had ever liked Marty?

Katani turned to Avery and Charlotte, who were sitting together. "There are plenty of cute dogs at the shelter that need a good home. Giving Marty to Robbie Flores would do a world of good for a lot of people."

Katani sat down. The room was eerily quiet.

"That was a very thoughtful plea, Katani," Ms. Rodriguez said. "But on the other hand, the love of a pet is a powerful thing. Animals can be like a part of the family."

Everyone in the room turned their heads to look at Avery and Charlotte.

"Man, if I were you, I'd take the money," Dillon said. "He already has the dog, right? So he has all the bargaining power. If you don't take the dough you might end up with nothing."

"We'll just see about that!" Avery growled. "I'll call every paper in Boston. I'll write a blog. Wait until everyone in the world finds out that Robbie Flores took a dog away from a group of kids." Avery rubbed her hands together with a mischievous twinkle in her eye and added, "We'll see who has bargaining power then!"

The bell rang and the students shuffled off to first-hour class. Ms. Rodriguez pulled Avery back from jogging out the door and called the BSG to her desk.

"I can see that you are all very emotional and upset about what happened over the weekend," Ms. R said in a calm, quiet voice. "You are all very creative individuals. I'm sure there's some type of solution. Why not put your heads together? All of you." She made eye contact with each of the girls as she spoke. "See what you can come up with."

"But Robbie Flores is leaving town tomorrow night," Avery protested.

"With Marty," added Charlotte. "It doesn't seem fair that he can do that. It's not even his dog. He just found him. We could call the police and my father said he would help me if that was what I wanted to do."

All the BSG stared at Charlotte. Calling the police would be a really big deal.

"Well, he's got to come back to Boston eventually, right?" Ms. Rodriguez asked.

"But he's going to Baltimore for a three-game series. He'll be gone for another week," Charlotte said. "With Marty."

"All the more reason for you to put your heads together now. Start working together instead of against each other," Ms. Rodriguez told them. "If you want to have a solution by tomorrow night, then make tomorrow night your deadline. Sometimes the pressure of a deadline helps sharpen your thinking and gets those creative juices flowing. Now get going, ladies. You have no time to lose!"

Katani held her stack of books tightly to her chest and rushed to her first-period class. She hated being late. Plus, she didn't feel like talking to her friends right now. What if they had seen right through her speech and knew the truth: She wanted the riding lessons to continue for herself as much as for Kelley. Katani felt ashamed and just wanted to go concentrate on something she could do well, like math.

Algebra was easy. You just had to follow the formula and it would usually come out right. *Why couldn't life be more like math?* she sighed.

LUNCH A BUNCH

Katani sat down at the BSG table, but she didn't even know where to begin. But neither did anyone else. The five friends began to eat in silence. It was Maeve who finally broke the ice.

She set down her milk with a small thud. Her friends looked up from their assorted yogurts and cafeteria cardboard sandwiches. "I've been thinking about our problem all day. Maybe Ms. Rodriguez has a point. Let's make tomorrow night our deadline. We can do this! We have to think of a solution. We're the BSG. We don't give up on each other. We stay loyal and we solve the problem."

The group stared at Maeve doubtfully.

"C'mon, girls, people have had to figure out harder problems than this!" Maeve said. "Remember *Titanic*? That was a serious deadline and a much bigger problem."

"Uh, Maeve?" Avery giggled. "Didn't the *Titanic* sink?"

"Well, there were *some* survivors."

Avery rolled her eyes and Katani finally melted. She let out a big Katani guffaw. Leave it to Maeve to break the ice with a movie reference!

"Maeve, you should definitely write a book someday," Katani said.

"*Moi?*" Maeve asked with an innocent look.

"Yes," Katani answered emphatically. "It should be called *Watch a Movie—Solve a Problem!*"

Maeve's face beamed. No one had ever suggested that she write a book before! She couldn't wait to tell her mother.

"We haven't exactly solved anything," the ever practical Avery interjected.

"True, but at least we have some hope now," Charlotte observed. "We just have to think about it some more."

"Maybe we should meet after school at Montoya's," Isabel suggested. "Nothing gets the ideas flowing like cookies and hot chocolate."

"Yum, I can taste those biscotti now!" Charlotte agreed. It was a date. Charlotte felt relieved. The BSG were together again. They would fix this and Marty would be home. She was convinced of it.

CHAPTER 19

ભ

SECOND CHANCE

THE SENTINEL OFFICE was located at the end of the hallway. It was a small room that had originally been used for storage before the students suggested that it would be perfect for the newspaper production. When Charlotte opened the door, she found Jennifer Robinson, eighth-grade editor of *The Sentinel*, at the computer sitting in a swivel chair. "You wanted to see me?" Charlotte asked.

Jennifer bit the end of her pencil and smiled. "You were interested in doing that piece on hurricane pets, right?"

Charlotte's breath caught in her throat. She tried not to look too excited. "Um, yes. I was. Why?"

"Good news," Jennifer said. "Today's your lucky day. You get to write the piece."

"I do?" Charlotte asked, scarcely able to believe her ears. She had dreamed about writing this story. It was right up her alley, all about volunteerism and animals. And Hilary Tamarack, the ninth-grade girl who worked at the shelter, was someone she truly admired. She couldn't wait to interview her and visit the animal shelter. "I'd love to,

Jennifer. What made you change your mind?"

Jennifer shrugged. "I just got tickets for the Red Sox game tonight. And since the deadline is Wednesday morning, I knew I just didn't have time to, you know, *really* dedicate myself to the piece," she said.

So that explained her sudden generosity. Charlotte had to smile. Jennifer was always looking out for numero uno. "But that doesn't leave me much time. I still have to set up an interview with Hilary Tamarack and visit the shelter and ..."

"No, you don't have to do any of those things. I already did that. Here are my notes from the interview." Jennifer looked pleased with herself.

Charlotte's felt her stomach turn. "What?"

"Here are my notes. It's everything you'll need to write the article."

Charlotte scanned the three sheets of paper that Jennifer had handed her. "But you didn't even visit the animal shelter. I thought the piece would be about—"

"Look, Charlotte. Are you gonna do it, or not?"

Charlotte wished she had the guts to tell Jennifer what she really thought. The idea for the piece had been her idea all along. Not even bothering to go to the shelter would make the story so much less interesting, but she was the reporter and Jennifer was the editor. She felt she had no choice. "I'll do it," Charlotte said quietly. Being a reporter was really frustrating sometimes.

"Well, that's good because if you don't do it, you can count on this being your last chance at the front page this year."

Charlotte scanned through the pages of notes again. "Did you ask her about—"

"Seriously, Charlotte!" Jennifer interrupted. "You can't just *re-interview* someone I've already interviewed! Do you know how bad that would look? Now just take the notes and write the article. I swear, it'll be fine."

Charlotte breathed deeply. She was really getting annoyed. She remembered what her father said, "Be polite, but stand up for yourself."

"But what about Ms. Rodriguez' lecture about keeping a reporter's notebook during *every interview*? What if she asks to see *my* notes from visiting the shelter?"

"Hey, you're the creative one. I'm sure you'll think of something," Jennifer said.

"But what about—"

"Really, Charlotte ... let it go!" Jennifer snapped. "You have all you need to write the piece. If necessary, I'll add details later."

"Add details later?" Charlotte asked. "How do you write an article without details?"

But her question fell on deaf ears. Jennifer had already left the room and headed to class.

Charlotte didn't look at Jennifer's notes again until the end of the day. The questions and answers were all very ordinary, run of the mill. Charlotte had been hoping that there would be something interesting, some fascinating tidbit that would really hook the reader. Charlotte stopped by the ninth-grade hall to see if she could find Hilary Tamarack and at least ask her a couple more questions. She ran into one of Hilary's friends, Julie Atkinson.

"Julie, Julie! Have you seen Hilary? I'm supposed to write an article about her for *The Sentinel* and I just need to ask her a few questions."

"Wait, didn't Jennifer tell you?"

"Tell me what?"

"Hilary's gone."

"What do you mean 'gone'?"

"Hilary's in Louisiana with her parents working with the animal rescue program. She won't be back until next week. She told me she wouldn't even have time to talk to me."

For the second time that day, Charlotte felt her stomach turn as she felt the harsh reality sink in. She had two days to write a cover story with shoddy notes, no details, no sources, and absolutely no way out. And she had to figure out how to convince Katani, Isabel, and Maeve that keeping Marty was the right thing to do. *Gosh,* thought Charlotte, *could things get any worse?*

HOT WATER

When Maeve arrived late to Montoya's, she was surprised to find that she was the first BSG there. She'd stayed after at the end of social studies, talking to Ms. O'Reilly about her last test. She had done better than she hoped, but Ms. O'Reilly wanted to show Maeve how she could improve her C grade to a B. By the time she made it to her locker, she didn't see any of the BSG and figured they'd all left for the bakery.

Mid-afternoon was usually a quiet hour at the bakery. Most kids had after-school activities and all the adults were at work. There were a few mothers with toddlers and a couple of elderly couples. On her way in she bent down to say hello to a curly-redheaded toddler. She explained to the mother than redheads had to stick together. Maeve sat down at a round table in the corner to finally catch her breath. She couldn't believe she had run the whole way for nothing

Eduardo, a cute college student who worked there in the afternoons and evenings, made his way to the table. He had a mop of curly, dark hair and deep, brown eyes as yummy as melted chocolate. "Hot chocolate, please," she said, when he asked what she wanted. Eduardo was very dreamy.

"Hey, where is everybody?" Isabel asked. She seemed just at breathless as Maeve as she collapsed in a chair.

"I don't know!" Maeve looked at her watch. "They should be here soon I hope …"

"To be honest, I'm glad it's just you right now. I wanted to talk to you about something, Maeve."

"Sure. What's up?"

Isabel sighed. "I feel so torn about Marty. I know how important he is to Charlotte and Avery, and I totally love the little guy but at the same time … I can't help thinking about the money. It could help so many people in so many ways. So then I wonder if it could be wrong to keep him."

"I know exactly how you feel," Maeve agreed as Eduardo brought the hot chocolate to the table. "I would hate to give up my little guinea pigs. It would just kill me. But if someone needed the money really bad I don't know how I would feel."

"Miss?" he asked looking at Isabel. She responded to him in Spanish and he nodded and walked back to the kitchen.

"What did you say?" Maeve asked.

"I told him that there would be three more of us coming in a minute, so he wouldn't have to make so many trips."

Charlotte arrived next, looking sad and downtrodden.

"Hey, Charlotte. Is everything … OK?" Maeve asked.

Charlotte blinked. "What? Oh. Yeah, I'm fine."

Maeve wanted to ask if there was anything going on—besides Marty missing of course—but before she could say anything, in tromped Avery followed by a somber Katani.

Eduardo returned to the table and Isabel ordered everyone a round of hot chocolate. An awkward silence hung over the group.

"OK," Maeve said. "Let's get started." She tried to keep her voice calm and confident. For a minute, she thought she actually sounded like Ms. Rodriguez. This made her sit a little taller. What would Ms. R do in this situation? She would probably ask everyone to write something down. It wasn't Maeve's favorite activity, but since no one seemed to want to talk, maybe writing was the best solution.

Maeve reached into her bag and pulled out a sheet of notebook paper. She folded it up and tore it into five strips. "OK, I have an idea. How about we all just write down what we want to happen?"

Considering the way the BSG had been getting along lately, Maeve expected *someone* to object. Surprisingly, though, the girls shrugged, nodded, and searched for their pencils. When everyone finished scribbling, Maeve tore another sheet into strips and handed them out again.

"Now write down what you think would be the best way to accomplish your goal," Maeve said.

Maeve wouldn't admit to anyone that she really didn't know what she was doing here. In fact, she had no plan at all. But she liked the fact that they were all in the same place, at the same table, attempting to solve the problem together. Something good was bound to happen.

"I'm going to collect the sheets now," Maeve said.

Maeve unfolded the papers, including her own, and read each of the goals:

- Save High Hopes Riding Stable
- Help people who need it
- Get Marty back
- Bring Marty home
- Make everybody happy

Even though no one had signed her name, it was pretty obvious who had written what. And she also could see that the group was hopelessly divided between the money and the dog. Maeve then asked everyone to pass in the next set of slips. The first one almost made her fall out of her chair.

"Kidnap Marty?" She read out loud. "Kidnap?"

"What's wrong with that?" Avery asked.

Maeve raised her eyebrows.

Katani snorted and looked at the ceiling. "Leave it to Avery to get us all arrested and put in prison. Read the next one, Maeve."

"Call Mr. Flores and accept his offer," Maeve read.

"That seems logical," Katani said but without the intensity of a few days ago.

Avery and Charlotte looked upset at her comment but neither wanted to say anything. When Katani had taken a position on something, they both knew it was hard to get her out of it. So, for once irrepressible Avery bit her tongue. Charlotte gave Avery a reassuring smile, which was the first time she had really reached out to Avery in days.

"Why don't you read the next one," Isabel suggested in a calm voice.

"Rent Marty to Mr. Flores for $10,000 a year during baseball season and then have Marty live with us the rest of the year," Maeve read and then looked at everyone with big eyes.

"Hey, that's not a bad idea," Katani said, suddenly upbeat.

"What?" Avery said. "Baseball season starts with spring training in February and continues through the end of October. That only leaves us eight weeks."

"Well, we've only had Marty a short time," Katani pointed out.

Avery was fuming. "Katani, I am so mad at you. You

only care about what you want to happen!" Katani looked stung and began to shift in her seat.

"OK, ENOUGH!" Maeve interrupted. "We still have more to read ..." She cleared her throat and held up another strip. "Convince Robbie Flores that Marty *isn't* his Lucky Charm so he will want to give him back."

The group looked at Charlotte.

"Belief is a powerful thing," said Isabel. "My mother's doctors talk about belief all the time. They say it always makes a difference if you believe."

"Sorry Charlotte, but that's never going to work."

Everyone jumped because no one realized that Nick had been listening to their conversation. Even Maeve, who had positioned herself so she could see everything in the room, had been so involved in the conversation that she didn't see him walk up to the table.

"What's not going to work?" Maeve asked.

"There's no way you can make Robbie Flores change his mind," Nick said.

"He'll change his thinking if I go to the press. The negative publicity will crush him," Avery said.

"Oh, that's great, Ave," Nick said. "The Sox are tied with the Yankees in first place with only four games left in the season. If Flores slumps and the team loses the next couple of games, it's over. Everyone in Boston will be protesting outside *your* house. Besides, do you really want *it* on your conscience that you took away the number-one Red Sox hitter's lucky charm?"

"Hey, we didn't ask him to steal our dog," Avery shot back.

"If I remember correctly, didn't he find Marty wandering around in a busy parking lot without a collar on? If he didn't take Marty that day, who knows what would have happened.

So don't blame Flores for trying to help a poor lost dog, Avery."

Nick's words were forceful. Charlotte kind of liked the daring gleam in his eyes, even if she didn't like everything he was saying. Nick's words had the opposite effect on Avery. She sank back into her chair and curled her head toward her chest.

Nick shook his head as he cleared the empty mugs from the table and disappeared behind the swinging doors.

"Baseball," Charlotte grumbled. "It's all people think about around here. Can we at least agree that Marty is more important than the Red Sox winning the series?"

That was definitely something all the BSG could agree on. Maeve tried to think of what Ms. Rodriguez would do now, but before she had a chance, Katani looked at her watch and said she had to get home.

"But we haven't finished solving this problem," a disappointed Maeve protested.

"I know but I have to be home. You know, Kelley …" Katani shrugged.

Where was Ms. Rodriguez when you really needed her? Maeve sighed.

Charlotte, Avery, and Isabel excused themselves as well.

Maeve sat at the table watching as her friends left Montoya's. She twirled a straw in her cocoa. Well, she thought, all things considered, the meeting could have gone worse.

CHAPTER 20

❧

WRITER'S BLOCK

"WHATCHA WORKING ON, Charlotte?" Mr. Ramsey asked.

Charlotte stared at the screen of her laptop. She had no idea how to get started on the article. She shut her eyes and tried to visualize what the shelter would have been like, but nothing came to mind. She was blank. No matter how hard she tried, Charlotte couldn't imagine the interview with Hilary or the animal shelter because she hadn't been there.

"Hey, Earth to Charlotte! Dad, here!"

At that moment, Charlotte could no longer hold it in. The tears that had been brimming in her eyes all day started trickling down her cheeks.

"I know. I know, honey," Mr. Ramsey said. "First Orangina and now Marty. Our track record isn't very good. It seems that when it comes to pets we aren't very lucky."

"It's not just that," Charlotte sniffled.

Her father lowered his eyebrows and looked perplexed. "It's not?"

"Marty is only part of it. I've had a really bad week. My friends and I can't agree on anything, and I don't know what we are going to do," she admitted.

"And that's only *part* of why you feel sad?" Mr. Ramsey asked. "What else?"

"Well, yesterday, Jennifer Robinson, the editor of *The Sentinel*, gave me this assignment for a front-page story."

"That's great, Charlotte!"

"No. NO! It's awful."

"Awful?" Mr. Ramsey looked more confused than before.

"Look at this!" Charlotte commanded, showing her father the three pages of notes. "How am I supposed to write a good piece from these notes? Jennifer said I can't call Hilary again and do a phone interview—she's in Louisiana right now. I haven't visited the shelter at all. Ms. Rodriguez keeps telling us to use detail, *telling* detail, and I can't do it! I feel like I'm trying to write from inside a paper bag."

"Nice analogy."

"Dad," Charlotte pleaded, "when I told Jennifer this afternoon that I didn't think I had enough information to write the piece, she told me not to worry about it. She already did the interview. She said I should just write the article with her notes and she'll add the details later."

"Hmm … that doesn't sound very helpful to me."

"I mean it's sort of like saying to an artist, go ahead and sketch that picture of the sunset in Arizona. Don't worry about the colors—we'll add them later."

Mr. Ramsey nodded. "I can see why you're frustrated. But as a writer you're going to have to learn how to deal with these situations. Being able to get firsthand observation and detail is the best, but when you can't, you have to learn to rely on other sources."

"This is almost like trying to design a house from a cartoon drawing."

"Another good analogy," Mr. Ramsey said with a smile. "But, it can be done. Remember when I was writing the book on the Great Barrier Reef? I really wanted to see a Great White Shark. After fifteen diving trips, I'd seen all kinds of sharks, but not a Great White. I had to rely on my experience with the sharks I did see and then supplement that with things other people told me."

Charlotte tried to recompose herself. "How can I do that here? I don't know anyone who works in a shelter."

"That's true, but you *have* lost a pet recently," Mr. Ramsey pointed out.

"What does that have to do with this?" Charlotte asked.

"You've been visiting lots of shelters lately. Not the shelter that Hilary volunteers at, but animal shelters all the same."

Charlotte thought back to the night when they went to the Sawgrass Animal Shelter when they thought they'd found Marty.

"Mix those firsthand thoughts and impressions with what you have here and I think you'll be able to get through this," Mr. Ramsey said.

Charlotte wiped away the last of her tears and took a deep breath. Sometimes her dad was so smart. She wished she hadn't waited so long to ask him for help. If she had asked earlier she wouldn't be so tired and frustrated.

"Writing is kind of like making a quilt," Mr. Ramsey continued. "It's a scrap craft. You take scraps of information, scraps of experiences—both your own and experiences of others. Then you cut and stitch until you put them together in a way that makes sense."

Charlotte threw her arms around her father's neck. "Thank you so much. This was really helpful."

"Honey, I wish I could solve the Marty problem just as

easily. Did you girls get any closer to a solution today?"

"No," Charlotte said, shaking her head. "We still have no idea what to do. Someone suggested renting Marty to Robbie Flores just for the baseball season. That almost seems like the best idea."

"Renting him?"

"Yeah. Marty could stay with Robbie Flores during baseball season and live with us the rest of the time. This year we could give the money to Katani's stable and next year maybe we could donate the money to the Multiple Sclerosis Society for Isabel's mom."

"You plan on charging $10,000 a season?"

"I know, I know. It does sound ridiculous. Do you think we'd be cheating him? I mean, you don't *really* believe that Marty is a good-luck charm, do you?"

Mr. Ramsey shrugged. "Well, that all depends on what Robbie Flores believes. Remember, belief is a powerful thing."

"That's exactly what Isabel said. It would be different if he gave us a donation for Katani's stable. But to take the money as payment for a *lucky charm* to win baseball games seems ... kind of crummy."

Mr. Ramsey looked at his watch. "Speaking of baseball, the game is starting now. Maybe we can do a little more research and see just how lucky this charm is," Mr. Ramsey suggested, clicking on the TV. Charlotte stretched out on the floor and tried to concentrate on writing her article as her father watched the game. It was easy to write during ball games because baseball didn't demand her full attention. All Charlotte had to listen for was the roar of the crowd and then watch the replay.

After two and a half hours, the Sox were down three to nothing. When the commercials came on, Mr. Ramsey leaned over and inspected Charlotte's notebook.

"How's it going, kiddo?" he asked.

Charlotte showed him the title. "Barlow Animal Shelter: A Home for Foul Weather Friends."

Mr. Ramsey read through Charlotte's rough draft during the bottom of the eighth. Neither of them was too worried about watching the game. It seemed the Sox were definitely going to lose this one.

Mr. Ramsey tapped the paper when he was done. "Good! Very good! And excellent detail. No one would know that you hadn't actually been there. Considering the circumstances, I'd say you did an outstanding job. See what happens when you use your imagination and your experience?"

Just then the crowd roared. Charlotte and her father turned their attention to the television.

"Look! Robbie Flores hit a grand slam homerun!" Mr. Ramsey exclaimed.

"Oh my goodness! The Red Sox won!" Charlotte shouted.

Mr. Ramsey slapped her five. "Maybe Marty is good luck! That was an incredibly lucky come back," he noted.

They heard a knock come from the bottom of the stairs. "Mr. Ramsey? Charlotte?" It was Miss Pierce, their landlady.

"I'm really sorry Miss Pierce. Are we too loud?" Mr. Ramsey asked.

"Heavens, no! I just finished watching the game myself. With a comeback like that who wouldn't be loud?"

Charlotte and her father breathed a sigh of relief as Miss Pierce continued, "I just thought you might be interested in what I found scratching at my back door." With that, she let go of the leash she was holding. Ten pounds of wiggling, jiggling mutt came bounding up the stairs.

"MARTY!" Charlotte screamed.

M.V.P. (MOST VALUABLE POOCH)

Marty was wearing a new red collar with a gold tag engraved with "Lucky Charm" in fancy letters.

"Oh, my!" Miss Pierce said when she saw that his mud-spattered body had gotten Charlotte's sweatshirt all muddy.

Marty jumped up and licked Charlotte's face, getting mud on her cheeks as well.

"How did he get here? He must have slipped away! You found your way home, didn't you, little guy? You smart little puppy!" Charlotte cried, hugging and kissing the little doggie all over. "Thanks so much, Miss Pierce."

"Now what are you going to do?" Mr. Ramsey asked.

"I have an idea," Charlotte replied. She picked up the phone and immediately called Avery to tell her the news.

"Now I can love baseball again! WHOOOO HOOO!" Avery yelled so loud, Charlotte had to hold the phone away from her ear. "When did you say that Marty showed up?" Avery asked.

"Just a few minutes ago, before Robbie Flores' homerun."

"Think about it, Charlotte. If Marty came home just now, he must have left Fenway a while ago, right? So ... Marty had nothing to do with the win!"

Charlotte gasped. "Which means that ..."

"MARTY ISN'T THE LUCKY CHARM!" Charlotte and Avery cried at the same time.

"If that's true, we can forget about the $10,000, I guess. Katani is going to be really disappointed," Avery reasoned.

Charlotte realized she was right. "I think maybe it would be a good idea if we waited 'til tomorrow and told the BSG in person."

"Agreed!" said Avery.

Just then, Charlotte thought of something. "Hey, Avery,

remember how scared we were when we couldn't find Marty? Do you think Robbie Flores is going through the same thing right now?" she asked.

"Maybe ..."

"I'd better call him."

"Charlotte, NO!" Avery exclaimed. "What if he wants to take him back?"

"Trust me," Charlotte said. "I don't think we'll have that problem."

When Charlotte told her father, he agreed that it was a good idea. She called the number that Robbie Flores left on her answering machine, but there was no answer. Flores' voicemail picked up the call.

Charlotte waited for the beep, then spoke. "Hi. This is Charlotte, one of the girls who owns Marty. I called to tell you that I know where he is ... Marty, that is ... I mean, Lucky Charm. Anyway, please call back," she said and left her number.

Charlotte was asleep when the phone rang at midnight.

"Hello?" she mumbled.

"This is Robbie Flores. I am going to the airport soon. Quick, please, I need my Lucky Charm. I can't go anywhere without him."

This was the moment Charlotte had been waiting for. "Mr. Flores, Marty isn't your lucky charm. He was already here when you hit your homerun tonight," Charlotte said.

There was stunned silence on the other end of the phone.

Charlotte had a flash of inspiration. She continued, "You are welcome to keep Happy Lucky Thingy, though."

"What?"

"You know, the little pink toy that Marty had when you found him?"

"*Si*," Mr. Flores replied.

"Well, if Marty was here when you won, *he's* not the lucky charm. It's Happy Lucky Thingy! That's the charm you've had the whole time!"

"You mean the toy, the one with the funny name, that is my lucky charm?" Robbie Flores asked.

"Exactly."

"My friend Katani is making you your own special Happy Lucky Thingy as we speak!" Charlotte crossed her fingers behind her back. "When you come back, we will have the most beautiful Happy Lucky for you."

"You know what? Maybe you're right! It was, how you say, *Happy Lucky Thingy*. Thank you, Charlotte. It is because of you and your friends that the Red Sox can win. I owe you all much. Please tell me what I can do to repay you for your help."

Charlotte paused. She called up her bravest self. "I'm really happy that Marty is back. And that you still have your lucky charm. So I guess we can both be happy. But some of my friends really wanted you to keep Marty. You see for them, the $10,000 would have made a big difference. My friend Katani's sister is autistic, and her therapeutic riding stable might have to close down. You know, the money would have been their lucky charm," she said. She absolutely couldn't believe that she managed to get her speech out. Her heart was pounding.

Charlotte briefly described the High Hopes Therapeutic Riding Program and the urgent need for funds. "I'm glad Marty came home, because we couldn't figure out how to work it out. But I know that Katani and Isabel would have been happy if things had been … different," she said. She bit her lip, unsure of what Robbie would do.

"I will think more about this. I must go now though— the plane is waiting for me. Thank you again Charlotte. Take good care of Lucky Charm … I mean, Marty. I'll miss that little dude."

Charlotte snuggled her face in Marty's wiggly little body.

Kgirl List:

1. *Look for other riding stable in reasonable driving distance from our house*
2. *Find out how much they cost*
3. *Figure out a way to convince mom and dad to pay for riding lessons*
4. *Figure out how many accessories I would have to sell in case mom and dad don't want to pay*

CHAPTER 21

◌

RED SOX FEVER

CHARLOTTE WOKE UP to something that had been missing for a long time: little wet kisses all over her face. Marty nuzzled into her chin and danced around on the bed until she got up and took him for a walk. This time she made sure his collar was on tight. Avery met her in the park and the two of them watched as the little dude checked in with his posse: Bella, Louie, Fly, Harley, Rosie, and of course, La Fanny. Marty did double flips for his friends and a great deal of barking and tail wagging ensued.

After returning Marty to the yellow Victorian, Charlotte rushed to gather up her backpack and books. She wanted to get to school early to turn in her article for *The Sentinel* before class started. While it wasn't the article she would have written if she had been in charge from the start, Charlotte was confident that with the information she'd researched it was the very best she could do. Besides, she knew that the sooner she left, the sooner she could tell the other BSG about Marty.

When Charlotte arrived at school, the halls were buzzing with excitement. Red Sox fever had hit Abigail Adams Junior

High big time. A group of eighth-grade girls were all wearing pink Red Sox T-shirts with their favorite players' numbers on the backs. Charlotte passed Pete and Dillon standing at their lockers dressed in white Red Sox team jerseys.

Before homeroom, Charlotte quietly told Ms. Rodriguez how Marty had found his way home. "That's incredible news!" Ms. R responded with a big smile. Charlotte wished that telling the rest of the girls would be so easy.

Despite the wild celebratory attitude in the halls, the BSG table was quiet at lunch. Charlotte definitely felt like she was the goose that swallowed the golden egg. Finally, she cleared her throat to get the girls' attention.

"Here ye, here ye!" Charlotte said, banging her chocolate milk carton on the table. No one laughed. "I have an important announcement."

The girls looked eagerly at Charlotte.

"Last night ... after the Red Sox game ... Miss Pierce came upstairs, and guess who she found?"

Charlotte let the suspense hang in the air, glanced sideways at Avery, then burst out, "MARTY!"

Maeve gasped. Isabel and Katani seemed stunned.

"Marty is back! Oh my goodness, are you serious?" Maeve cried.

"Wait a minute, what does this mean?" asked Isabel. "Did Robbie Flores give him back?"

Katani's voice trembled as she spoke. "Did you tell him that we didn't want the money? I thought we were going to agree first!" she exclaimed.

Avery jumped out of her chair. "No, silly, Marty found his way home all by himself!"

"I called Robbie Flores and told him," Charlotte added. "Marty was not at Fenway when Robbie hit the grand slam.

I convinced Robbie that Happy Lucky Thingy was the real lucky charm. He's says he wants to repay us. I'm not sure what that means, exactly."

"I'll tell you exactly what it means," Katani blurted out. "Six tickets to a Sox game AT BEST. Let's face it ... we can forget about saving the stable. But then, I guess you all weren't really worried about it in the first place." Katani abruptly got up and left the group.

Charlotte was completely flabbergasted. She didn't even get to tell her story before Katani bolted. Avery muttered something about catching up on the game with the guys and left as well.

Charlotte explained to Isabel and Maeve what happened. While both girls were genuinely thrilled that Marty was safe back home, there was an uncomfortable silence around the reward. Especially when Isabel found out that Charlotte had given up the $10,000 reward and expected Katani to make a new Happy Lucky Thingy for Robbie Flores.

"But," Charlotte defended herself, "I told him that the stable needed money, and he said he was going to think about making a donation."

"Well," Maeve exclaimed. "Why didn't you tell us this in the first place?"

"I was getting to it, but then Katani left in such a huff ..." Charlotte put her hand up to stop Maeve from jumping in. "Look, I know she was upset and I am going to go find her and explain. I promise. I don't want her to feel hurt anymore."

Avery had spent most of her lunch hour at the boys' table, laughing and talking about last night's fantastic come-from-behind Red Sox win. Bits and pieces of the conversation floated over to the BSG table.

Charlotte thought perhaps Avery had the right idea of

staying at the boys' table. She wished Robbie Flores had never offered them that enormous reward in the first place. Then they could be celebrating Marty's return instead of wondering what might have been.

Maeve consoled Charlotte later that day at her locker. "You didn't make the decision, Charlotte. Marty did, when he came back to you. You can't help the way things turned out."

"Tell that to Katani. Marty's return means her miracle bubble has burst."

"Give her time," Maeve said. "Listen, I have an idea. Why don't we throw Marty a homecoming party on Saturday? Katani would come to that, wouldn't she?"

Charlotte shrugged. She wasn't sure that Katani would forgive her now ... or ever.

"Fabulous! Now I don't want you to worry about the matter anymore. Things will work out OK," Maeve assured her. Charlotte had to laugh. Charlotte wondered what any of the BSG would do without their lively, redheaded, movie-obsessed friend.

When Charlotte got home, the first thing she tried was calling Katani, but her mother said she was in her room working on some project and didn't want to be disturbed.

Charlotte checked her computer throughout the night hoping that Katani was online. She was not. Time for a global perspective, Charlotte determined.

To: Sophie
From: Charlotte
Subject: Marty

Sophie-

You were right. Marty found his way home.
But my problems aren't over. The man who
found him wanted to keep him. And he
offered $10,000! Isabel and Katani wanted
to keep the money—for good reasons. Now
that Marty ran away from him and came
back to me the deal is off. I'm afraid
Katani will never forgive me for this
chance at so much money. Katani is
really, really upset.
I wish things could be like they were
before Marty ran away.
Charlotte

Avery's Blog

Call off the search!
Marty returned!
He arrived at Charlotte's house last night just in time to see
Robbie Flores' game winning, grand slam homerun!
Homecoming party planned for Saturday night.
Promise I'll post pictures of the big event on Sunday morning!

CHAPTER 22

☙

FOWL WEATHER

AS SOON AS CHARLOTTE walked through the doors of Abigail Adams Junior High on Thursday morning, she knew there was something weird going on.

"Cluck, Cluck CLUCK," Pete Wexler said. He folded his arms back, placing his fists in his arm pits and flapping his arms like they were wings. "Cock-a-doodle-doo!" he crowed.

The crowd of kids around him collapsed into laughter, although some of them flapped their arms like wings and clucked and crowed too.

"Good morning, Peter," Charlotte said as she passed him. "I guess."

As Charlotte made her way down the hall to homeroom, several other groups of people flapped their arms as if they were chicken wings and made bird noises at her.

Then someone grabbed her elbow from behind.

Startled, Charlotte turned around. "Jennifer!" she cried. "What's up?"

Jennifer glared at Charlotte as if she were an irritating bug she planned on squashing at any moment. "If you try to pin this on me I'll deny everything," Jennifer snarled.

"What are you talking about?" Charlotte sputtered.

Jennifer let go of her elbow and said breathlessly, "Listen. You can't win this one. You didn't have a tape recorder anyway. If you just admit your mistake ..." Jennifer broke into a strange smile, "I'm sure this whole little scandal will clear itself up." Charlotte opened her mouth to ask what was going on, but Jennifer already took off down the hall.

What was THAT about? Charlotte wondered as she continued down the hall. Maeve was at Charlotte's locker and immediately gave her a hug.

"It's OK, Charlotte. Believe me, I know *all* about making stupid spelling mistakes. When you have dyslexia it happens all the time. In fact, I didn't even notice it until someone pointed it out to me," Maeve mentioned.

"Pointed what out?" Charlotte asked.

"Oh, my gosh! You don't know? OK, darling, brace yourself," Maeve said as she handed Charlotte a copy of *The Sentinel*, hot off the presses.

Charlotte unfolded the paper.

The title of her front-page article read in large print:

Barlow Shelter: Home for Fowl Weather Friends.

"Fowl Weather Friends? FOWL WEATHER! But I didn't write 'fowl' I wrote 'foul'. Really! I did!" Charlotte insisted.

Maeve didn't say anything. She placed her hand on Charlotte's shoulder as if to let her know she understood.

Charlotte didn't have time to explain any further. The bell rang and the two girls scurried to class.

When Charlotte entered the classroom, she avoided Ms. Rodriguez. She couldn't look at Ms. R after what had happened. She was just so ashamed. She went to her seat and pretended to read her day planner.

English class was a blur—Charlotte couldn't remember what they learned or discussed. Just after the bell rang, Ms. Rodriguez motioned Charlotte toward her.

Charlotte timidly made her way to her teacher's desk. "Yes?" she asked, staring at her shoes.

"Charlotte, Jennifer has accepted responsibility for the mistake in the paper. After all, copyediting is her job. But she also told me that you turned the article in late. She didn't have time to give it the proper proofreading that was necessary." Ms. Rodriguez said. "I am a little disappointed, Charlotte. Can you tell me what happened?"

Charlotte wanted to sink through the floor. She couldn't even look at Ms. R. If she defended herself, she would sound like a whiner. So she said nothing.

SABOTAGED

"I'll never write again," Charlotte said to the girls at lunch. "I have to quit the newspaper."

"Isn't that a little extreme?" Maeve asked.

"Quitters never win and winners never quit," Avery added knowingly.

"Look, Charlotte, we all make mistakes …" Maeve started.

"But it wasn't a mistake. I think Jennifer did it on purpose," Charlotte said softly.

Maeve looked puzzled. "Jennifer seems so nice. Are you sure?"

"I don't know," Isabel said. "I think Charlotte might be right. Ever since that meeting last week, Jennifer has been acting really weird. It's like I said—I think she's kind of jealous of Charlotte. Maybe this was her way of getting even."

"By purposely misspelling a word?" Maeve asked.

"No, it's worse," Charlotte said. "Did you read this? She

totally messed up my article. She added all these random things. She ruined the whole flow of the piece and her phrasing sounds awkward. It's not even close to the article I turned in. The worst part of all is that *my* name's on this. People think I actually wrote this!"

"I think you should talk to Jennifer. Confront her," Katani said.

Charlotte shook her head. "This morning in the hall she told me I can't win this one. I mean, what's the point? She's the editor! I don't have a chance. If I drop out, then next year when she's at high school, I can be on the staff again."

"Stop writing?" Maeve asked. "Pffft. Writing isn't what you do, it's who you ARE! Besides, we need you! The BSG and all the seventh graders! You fought hard to get seventh graders on the staff, and now everyone loves your work. You can't give it up because of one misspelled word."

"Maeve, it wasn't just a misspelled word. It's the whole article. Something went really wrong here. I'm afraid that as long as Jennifer is editor, there's going to be trouble for me," Charlotte admitted.

Katani tapped Charlotte on the arm. "My riding instructor says when you fall off a horse it's important to get right back in the saddle. That's what you have to do."

Charlotte smiled, relieved that Katani was offering her advice. Katani had been touched that Charlotte had been brave enough to ask Robbie Flores for the money. As a result, Katani was hard at work on a new Happy Lucky Thingy and was hoping against hope that Robbie would be so grateful that he would offer a donation to save the riding stable.

"Katani, how do I write another article without Jennifer interfering?" Charlotte asked. She was happy to take Katani's advice. The Kgirl was really good at problem solving when she put her mind to it. Her executive, take-charge manner might be just what the doctor ordered.

"Write about something you are passionate about," Katani suggested. "Something you have the inside scoop on."

"Katani's right. You should do it," Isabel said.

"I can write it, but that doesn't mean Jennifer will publish it," Charlotte said. "And it also doesn't mean she won't put her own twist on it."

"Then don't let her! Write for a different paper instead!" Katani exclaimed. "*The Sentinel*'s not the only game in town. We'll read your story. We'll act as editors and then you can send it to the *Beacon Street News*, the town newspaper. They take articles from kids!"

Charlotte was thrilled. Writing for the town newspaper gave her a feeling of exhilaration. She left lunch feeling better about her *fowl* article, even though kids were still flapping their wings and making chicken noises at her. In fact, when Kiki Underwood walked by and made a chicken sound, Charlotte put her nose in the air and quacked right back. Nick Montoya happened to walk by right then and he told her that she was a "cool bird."

That evening, Charlotte put all her energy into writing. She was glad she had taken her notebook everywhere with her in the past week. It was full of great ideas and lots of details. As Ms. Rodriguez had said, good writing begins in the notebook.

She showed her father her finished article before she went to bed. "This is great, honey," he said. "Really great! Is this for the next issue of *The Sentinel*?"

Charlotte told her father about the "fowl" turn of events, the heckling she'd endured from classmates and the reprimand she'd received from Ms. Rodriguez. "I really thought I would

"Who's Penelope?"

"My point exactly. Penelope is my horse that I ride. I love her and you don't even know who she is," Katani said.

"It's not Marty's fault," Charlotte reasoned.

"It's not anyone's fault," Isabel added.

"I know," Katani said. "I just think it's going to be hard for me to be around Marty again, knowing I'll never be able to see Penelope."

Avery opened her mouth, but nothing came out. She suddenly understood just how Katani felt. Avery wanted to meet Penelope too.

"Please come, Katani," Isabel said, putting her hand on Katani's arm.

"You have to come," Maeve told her. "It won't be the same without you."

"Besides," Charlotte told her. "I finished that piece—the one you encouraged me to write. You promised to be my audience. I really want you to read it."

Katani smiled in spite of herself. "Yeah. It has been a while since we've had an overnight. I'll think about it. I have a riding lesson after school. My last. I don't know if I could love any horse as much as I do Penelope," Katani said.

HOPE-LESS?

"Are you girls ready?" Grandma Ruby asked as she drove the girls to the stable after school.

When Grandma Ruby turned on the familiar road to High Hopes, Katani's heart sank. This was probably the last day she'd ever see Penelope. She tossed the apple she'd brought for Penelope back and forth in her hand. She was out of hope today.

Grandma Ruby looked back at Katani in the rearview

mirror. "Hey, can you turn your frown upside-down, Katani? You'd think I was driving you to a funeral. I thought you liked riding lessons."

Katani nodded and gave her grandmother a weak smile.

"Why are you sad, Katani?" Kelley asked. "I love Wilbur. I thought you loved Penelope too."

"I do love Penelope, Kelley," Katani said. Kelley grabbed her hand as Katani looked out the car window and whispered, "That's why I'm so sad …"

When they pulled up to the stable, things already seemed different. No one was doing chores around the fence. There weren't any horses in the corral. Katani wondered if they had decided to close down the stable early.

"Something is wrong," Kelley said. "Maybe one of the horses is sick."

When Big Blue ground to a halt, Katani slowly opened her door and walked toward the stable. Samantha was the first out the stable door, quickly followed by Catherine.

"There they are!" Catherine shouted. "Claudia, look, they're here!"

"Thank you! Thank you! Thank you!" Samantha said. She plowed into Katani and gave her a huge hug.

"For what?" Katani asked.

Catherine laughed. "For what? Like you don't know!"

Claudia walked out of the stable and waved.

Katani waved back.

"So I guess I owe you about five years of private lessons," Claudia said.

"You do? Why?"

Claudia looked at Catherine, who was still beaming. Catherine shrugged and shook her head.

"Ahem. Katani, Robbie Flores donated ten thousand

dollars to High Hopes in your little dog's name," Claudia said.

Katani suddenly felt dizzy. "Excuse me?" she murmured.

"Better yet, he and his teammates have agreed to sponsor a fundraiser over the winter to establish an ongoing foundation to keep the program running. *Forever*."

Kelley tapped Catherine on the shoulder. "I can ride Wilbur for a long time?" Kelley asked.

"For a very long time," Claudia said.

Kelley cheered.

In Katani's daze, it occurred to her that she was smiling. And it occurred to her that both Claudia and Catherine were calling her name. "Katani? Hello, Katani?" Claudia called.

"What? Yes?"

"Just one teeny, tiny question. How on Earth were you able to get the Red Sox to donate time and money to the stable?" Claudia asked.

The group had begun to make their way over to the stable. Miracle or no miracle, someone had to curry the horses.

Katani thought before she spoke. "It wasn't me," Katani explained. "One of my best friends made this happen. Would there be any way you guys could help me with a little thank you gift?"

Claudia laughed. "For the girl who saved the stable? Anything. You name it."

Katani nodded and ran ahead to the barn. She couldn't wait to be reunited with Penelope. Apparently Penelope felt the same way. She nuzzled right against Katani's cheek with her soft nose.

Katani loved trotting around the ring with Penelope that day more than any other. Katani hugged Penelope and buried her face in her neck. "We'll get to be together for a long, long time. I know we will," she whispered into Penelope's ear.

✿

To: Katani
From: Isabel
Subject: Saturday's Party

Katani-

i know u r disappointed. me 2. i thought
the ≠≠≠≠ might be the answer to lots of
my problems. But, what if Marty had never
gotten lost ... things would be the same
as they are now. Only no one would be mad
or hurt.
Don't give up what you have now—great
friends—because of something you might
have had.
Please come!
Isabel

଼

CHAPTER 24

HOMECOMING PARTY

ISABEL HEARD A KNOCK on Charlotte's front door. "I'll get it!" she cried.

"Thank you!" Charlotte called from the kitchen. She and Mr. Ramsey were busy in the kitchen making pizzas for Marty's homecoming party. Isabel bounced down the grand stairway of the old Victorian home on Corey Hill. Since Katani hadn't returned her email, Isabel expected to see Maeve or Avery.

She opened the door to find Katani standing there, looking radiant, and carrying two large bags. "Katani!" she shouted and quickly hugged her friend. "I'm so happy to see you! Thank you for coming," Isabel said, squeezing Katani's hand.

"Are you kidding? I wouldn't have missed this for the world!" Katani said.

Isabel raised an eyebrow doubtfully.

Katani smiled. "OK, maybe I *almost* missed this for the world. But the point is, I didn't!" The girls laughed and embraced again.

"Let me carry one of your bags," Isabel said. "Oof! This

is heavy? What do you have in here? Rocks?"

"You'll see," Katani said mysteriously.

"Who is it?" Charlotte called down as they started up the stairs.

"You'll never guess!"

"Robbie Flores?" Charlotte asked devilishly.

"Ha ha," Isabel said.

"Katani!" Charlotte screeched when Katani reached the top of the stairs. "I'm so glad you came! It wouldn't have been the same without you!"

"I'm glad to be here," Katani said. "If you don't mind, I'm going to take my things up to the Tower now."

"Want any help with this one?" Isabel asked.

Katani put one finger over her lips so Isabel would know not to say anything about the bag. Isabel nodded and helped carry it to the top of the ladder.

"Here you go," Isabel said, setting the bag on the floor.

"Thanks," Katani said. "I'll take it from here. Thanks for not saying anything about it. It's a surprise."

"Just having you here is surprise enough for me," Isabel replied softly.

By the time Katani made it down from the Tower, Avery and Maeve had arrived. Both were delighted to see that Katani had joined the party.

After everyone snarfed down homemade pizza and salad, Mr. Ramsey built a fire in the living room fireplace, and the girls toasted marshmallows and made s'mores—a favorite BSG tradition.

"Ready on three," Isabel prompted. "One ... two ... three!"

"Thank you for dinner, Mr. Ramsey," the girls sang out in unison.

"We're going up to the Tower now Dad," Charlotte said.

"Marty too, of course!" Avery added. "After all, he's the guest of honor."

"Good night, ladies," Mr. Ramsey said. "And try to get a little sleep. It's called a *slumber* party for a reason."

"Technically, it's a welcome home party for Marty," Charlotte reminded him. "But we'll consider sleeping, I guess."

Up in the Tower, the true homecoming party began.

Avery had made a banner and got Marty to do all his tricks. She was happy to discover he hadn't forgotten a single one. He even remembered how to give her a high five.

"Or paw five, as I like to call it," Avery laughed.

Maeve had borrowed the huge picture of Marty dressed as Klondike Pink for the Dress-Your-Pet-in-Pink contest at Think Pink.

"OK, girls," Charlotte said. "I have some news."

"Me too," Katani said.

"OK, Katani, you first," Charlotte insisted.

"Well, my news is about High Hopes," Katani said.

"The riding stable?" Isabel asked.

"Or literally ... high hopes?" Maeve asked.

"Both ... sort of." Katani reached into one of the enormous bags she had brought. "I have something for each of you. I hope that your high hopes will come true today, so I made a 'lucky charm' for each of you."

Isabel laughed as Katani produced a horseshoe. "That's why they were so heavy!" Isabel exclaimed.

Katani had personalized each horseshoe by painting each BSG's name in bright pink letters and the phrase "May all your high hopes come true." She had adorned the writing with designs to fit all of her friends: notebooks and pencils for Charlotte, dance shoes and musical notes for Maeve, paintbrush and easel for Isabel, and baseballs for Avery—

with the word "Red Sox."

"Look at these. I can't believe you did all this work, Katani!" Charlotte exclaimed.

"A Red Sox horseshoe?" Avery cried. "Sweeeeet! One of a kind by the Kgirl!"

Maeve held hers close to her heart. "I'll treasure this forever," she said softly.

Katani looked at Charlotte. "I have *you* to thank for what happened," Katani told her.

"Why, what happened?" Isabel asked.

"Now, I'm curious," Katani continued. "What exactly *did* you say to Robbie Flores?" she asked Charlotte.

"I don't know … what do you mean?" Charlotte sputtered.

"Whatever it was, it must have been pretty convincing, because he wrote a check for $10,000 to High Hopes."

The girls stared with open mouths.

"They won't have to close after all!" Katani shrieked.

"Are you kidding? I don't believe it!" Charlotte shouted.

"Get OUT!" Avery shouted. "This is completely amazing. A-MAZING!"

Katani retold the whole story of arriving at the stable Friday afternoon expecting it to be her last riding lesson.

"That's why I asked for the lucky horseshoes. I wanted you all to have a lucky charm for your high hopes," Katani said.

"Well, now I have some news. Katani, I think your good luck has already worked for me! I have something for each of you too," Charlotte said. She went over to the desk and returned with a pile of papers. She handed each girl a copy of the *Beacon Street News*. "Turn to the sports section, page 5," Charlotte instructed them.

Avery was the first to find the article. "Wow! Look at this! 'Lucky Charms Power Baseball,' by…" Avery gasped.

"CHARLOTTE RAMSEY!" Avery said.

"You said I should write something for you guys, Katani. I hope you don't mind if everyone else in the neighborhood reads it as well," Charlotte said.

Everyone was quiet as they read the article.

"This is awesome," Maeve pronounced.

"I guess I have you to thank, Katani, and your advice to 'get back in the saddle.' I decided to write an article about baseball players' superstitions. And since I had Robbie Flores' cell phone number ..."

"You go, girl!" Katani shouted out.

"I called Robbie Flores and interviewed him over the phone. He told me lots of details about his teammates' superstitions," Charlotte reported.

"This is so cool," Avery said, looking at the article again.

"By the way, Mr. Flores also said that everything worked out great for him. When he arrived in Baltimore they made a big point to tell him that dogs weren't allowed in the ballpark. He wouldn't have been able to take Marty on the road to a lot of the dugouts after all. So now he thinks that his real lucky charm is Happy Lucky Thingy. That's probably why he sent the check to High Hopes, don't you think?" Charlotte wondered.

"Probably," Katani agreed.

"It's a great article, Charlotte. But, how did it end up in a real, live newspaper?" Isabel asked.

"Dad knows the editor. He emailed him my article. I got a check in the mail the next day," Charlotte added.

"You got paid for this?"

"Yup. And the editor called this evening to say that AP picked up the story. It's going to be in newspapers across the nation starting tomorrow," Charlotte said proudly.

"You're famous!" Maeve shouted.

Charlotte blushed. "Well, I wouldn't go *that* far. But it is pretty cool."

"So does that mean you're not quitting *The Sentinel*?" Isabel asked.

"I'm staying. Dad suggested that I turn this article into Ms. Rodriguez first."

"Phew! I'd miss you too much!" Isabel said.

"And I have something for you, Isabel," Charlotte said.

"For me?" Isabel asked. She was stunned.

Charlotte handed Isabel an envelope. Isabel opened it and pulled out a thin slip of paper. It was a check.

Isabel felt faint. "What? No ... I could never accept this," she murmured.

"No arguments, please. I'm signing it over to you. It's not much, but you can use it for whatever you like. Maybe it will help fly your father here for Christmas, or you could get something extra special for your mom, or if you want, you can donate it to the MS Society."

Isabel's throat swelled up with emotion. "Charlotte ... this is your first paycheck for writing. It's too much."

Charlotte shook her head. "If I've learned anything in the last few days it's that the support and love of friends is much more important than money. Money is only worth something when it can be spent on the good of all," Charlotte said.

Marty jumped in her lap and yapped loudly.

"See? Even Marty agrees," Charlotte said with a laugh.

Isabel hugged Charlotte. "Thank you," she whispered. "This means so much."

Soon the other three joined in.

"Group hugs for all," Maeve cheered.

"It's all for one," Avery shouted.

"And one for all," Katani finished.

"Yap Yap!" Marty barked.

The BSG were back in business.

"OH, before I forget." Katani went to her bag. She turned and proudly displayed her handiwork. A new Happy Lucky Thingy—all pink and clean and definitely not smelly!

CR

To be continued ...

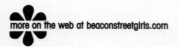

New BSG special adventure!

charlotte in paris

Charlotte returns to Paris to search for her long lost cat and to visit her best Parisian friend, Sophie. When a stolen Picasso sketch ends up in Charlotte's backpack, the BSG's bon voyage gifts become the detective tools for solving the mystery.

 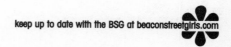

lucky charm Book Extras

Book Club Buzz

5 QUESTIONS FOR YOU AND YOUR FRIENDS TO CHAT ABOUT

1. Why is Marty so special to the Beacon Street Girls?

2. What happens to the effort to bring Marty home when the BSG begin to fight?

3. Why do you think Kelley and other kids with autism find horses so soothing?

4. Why is Charlotte so distraught about losing Marty?

5. Do you believe in lucky charms? Do you have one?

more *Lucky Charm* Book Club Buzz at beaconstreetgirls.com

Charlotte Ramsey

Charlotte's Word Nerd Dictionary

BSG Words

Phenom: (p. 25) noun—slang for "phenomenon" … a remarkable or exceptional person
Fabulosity: (p. 141) adjective—extra fabulous in Maeve's world

Other Cool Words …

Torrent: (p. 7) noun—a rushing, violent stream of water
Relent: (p. 17) verb—to become more mild, compassionate, or forgiving
Impassioned: (p. 19) adjective—filled with intense feeling or passion
Salient: (p. 22) adjective—important
Nonchalant: (p. 23) adjective—coolly unconcerned
Circulate: (p. 23) verb—to move in a circle or circuit
Hippotherapy: (p. 28) noun—medical treatment using movement of a horse
Dejected: (p. 51) adjective—depressed in spirits; disheartened

Optimistic: (p. 55) adjective—tending to look on the more favorable side of events or conditions

Analogy: (p. 60) noun—making a comparison between like features of unlike things

Tangent: (p. 78) noun—changing suddenly from one course of action or thought to another

Curry: (p. 79) verb—to rub and clean a horse with a currycomb

Reprieve: (p. 82) noun—the state of being relieved temporarily

Summon: (p. 90) verb—to call into action; rouse

Cacophony: (p. 97) noun—harsh mix of sound

Altercation: (p. 120) noun—a heated or angry dispute

Objectivity: (p. 122) noun—not influenced by personal feelings; unbiased

Crestfallen: (p. 174) adjective—dejected; discouraged

Agog: (p. 185) adjective—highly excited, as in anticipation

Guffaw: (p. 189) verb—a loud, unrestrained burst of laughter

Definitions adapted from *Webster's Dictionary*, Fourth Edition, Random House.

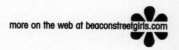

lucky charm **trivialicious trivia**

1. Who plays a mean trick on Charlotte when she writes her article for *The Sentinel*?
    A. Miss Pierce
    B. Maeve
    C. Jennifer Robinson
    D. Ms. Rodriguez

2. How much money does Robbie Flores offer the BSG for Marty?
    A. $1,000,000
    B. $5,000
    C. $50,000
    D. $10,000

3. What is the name of Kelley's horse at High Hopes?
    A. Penelope
    B. Charlotte
    C. Wilbur
    D. Pokemon

4. What does Marty have with him when he is found by Robbie Flores?
    A. A bone
    B. Happy Lucky Thingy
    C. $20
    D. Fleas

5. Who brings Marty back to the Ramseys?
    A. Robbie Flores
    B. Miss Pierce
    C. Anna and Joline
    D. Happy Lucky Thingy

ANSWERS: 1. C. Jennifer Robinson **2. D.** $10,000 **3. C.** Wilbur **4. B.** Happy Lucky Thingy **5. B.** Miss Pierce